For Beverley and Hazel

Chapter One

It began when Sam Williams decided to stay awake all night.

This wasn't something he would have thought of doing if he had been on his own. But Hannah, Amy and Dean were there too. They were fed up with watching TV and were in the mood for a challenge.

Hannah started it. She began by wondering what would happen if they didn't sleep at all.

'You'd probably get tired and then reach a point where you didn't get any more tired, and then you'd begin to wake up.'

Hannah always sounded as if she knew everything, and Sam, Dean and Amy thought she probably did. Her nose was always in a book and they all reckoned her thick glasses came from too much reading. Plus both of Hannah's parents were teachers. Sam, Dean and Amy privately felt very sorry for her.

'I bet *you* couldn't stay up all night,' Dean challenged her.

Hannah glanced at him contemptuously and helped herself to some more crisps from the bowl on the floor. Amy did the same.

'I bet *you* couldn't,' Hannah said.

It was enough. Within a few moments all four of them had decided not to go to sleep. There was no point telling Sam's mum, as naturally they were going to keep very quiet, have the telly on low and surprise her in the morning. They didn't want to disturb her because she had been working hard all day, getting ready for the new lodger, who was due to arrive soon.

When Sam thought back, he remembered little of that night, except it was much less fun than he had thought it would be. They talked for some time about school, about kids they knew, about this and that. Hannah got into her lecturing mode and explained why it was they were all friends.

'Because nobody else likes us. We don't fit in. People call me bossy even though I'm only trying to help. Dean can't stay still—'

'Yes, I can!' Dean shouted, and froze like a statue for a second or so.

'Amy won't speak to anyone else except us, and as for you – you're too nice for a boy, Sam.'

Sam knew what she meant and it made him uncomfortable. He was aware of having what his mother called a soft side. When he was little he had thought it meant he would bruise easily, but now he realised it was that he always found himself sticking up for the victims in fights, taking pity on any number of waifs and strays, and secretly – so secretly that not even Hannah knew this – crying in sad films. It was because sometimes Sam could feel what other people were going through, almost as if their feelings were in his head. But that was something he kept very much to himself. He had worked out that in Year 7 at Park Place Community School having a soft side wasn't going to get you very far, so he was trying to toughen up. Perhaps staying awake all night would be a beginning.

After Hannah had outlined what was wrong with each of them, they laid into her and there was a cushion fight which only ended when Sam's mum came down and told them all to shut up.

Then Hannah sat on the floor hugging a cushion and Amy copied her. Dean said they ought to each tell the scariest story they knew. He began with a complicated tale of a vampire city in Transylvania, but everyone lost interest because there were too many vampires and they couldn't work out which was which. Hannah told them a story about a prisoner in a shrinking room with spikes on the walls that had them all looking nervously at Sam's mum's white woodchip wall-paper. Sam came next with a story he remembered about a coachman with no face who waylaid stranded travellers on the moor. He caught Dean yawning once or twice.

It was Amy's turn. She was quiet for a while and everyone thought she'd duck out. But she didn't.

'My mother says there really are ghosts,' she said. 'The dead never leave us.'

'Amy!' said Hannah warningly. 'Remember, Sam's grandma died recently.'

Sam didn't need reminding. He'd thought that as soon as Amy had spoken. He didn't know whether he liked the idea that Grandma was still knocking about or hated it, because everyone reckoned ghosts were scary. His mind wandered then, to think what his grandma would have to say about his mum clearing out her room and refitting it for a lodger, the same lodger who was moving in the next day – after which there would be no more sleepovers, at least not in this house.

'I don't think you ought to tell a story about a ghost, Amy. I don't think it's tactful.'

Sam worried that Amy would stop talking altogether now. It was a problem to get her to speak at the best of times. At school she hardly said a word, and the teachers pestered her about it all the time. The more they went on at her, the quieter she became. Once he had heard Hannah's mum refer to her as an 'elective mute'. Which was better than calling her Chinky or Slitty Eyes, which was what some of their class did.

Amy was not put off by Hannah's remark, but carried on.

'Do you know what a zombie is?' she asked.

'One of the living DEAD!' Dean exclaimed.

'A dead body,' Amy went on, 'inhabited by a wicked living spirit.'

All of them were silent.

'A zombie seems alive, but isn't. So some-one sitting next to you on the bus might be a zombie. You can tell by looking in their eyes. They have a flat, yellow look. Like cats' eyes. You could meet a zombie on the bus and think he was normal – he might be wearing a brown suit, a tie with a crest on it, brown polished shoes – but if you accidentally touched his skin, it would be ice cold, and you could feel the bones underneath.'

'What do zombies do?' Dean asked, but now in a hushed tone.

'They want to destroy us. They're controlled by a demon who plans to take over the world from the forces of good. He'll reclaim the dead and fill them with his spirits. Then there'll be more of them than there are of us, all thinking and feeling the same, doing the same things, doing what they're told. All the time. And we must either be like them or fight back.'

'How do you fight a zombie?' Dean asked. His thumb had slipped into his mouth.

'Amy, where do you get such weird stories from?' Sam asked her. Only he *knew* the answer. She was always making up strange stuff. Their teacher once told the class that Amy had the strangest imagination he'd ever come across. That hadn't been a kind thing to say. Maybe that was why Amy never talked in school.

'I know about vampires too,' Amy continued. 'They—'

'This is boring!' Hannah declared. 'Let's put the telly back on. Or have something else to eat. Got any more crisps, Sam?'

Sam went to look in the kitchen, deciding that Hannah was genuinely scared by Amy's story. He wasn't surprised. He felt a little shaken too, but he put that down to the fact it was way past the time he'd usually go to sleep. In the morning he'd laugh about zombies. He'd probably jump on Hannah when she wasn't looking, chanting, 'I am a zombie,' and they'd both have a good giggle. But not now. Now he'd hunt around for some more crisps. Funny, though. He'd never seen Hannah scared before.

The night passed slowly. Around three in the morning Amy and Hannah started arguing about something or other and both of them ended up in tears, and it was Sam who had to sort it out. Dean went very quiet and just sat, glassy-eyed, in a corner. Like a zombie, Sam thought. Sam battled against tiredness as best he could. He felt a delicious warmth stealing along his arms and up his legs. His legs became heavy. More than anything he wanted to close his eyes, just for a moment, but he knew that if he did, he'd be lost. He sat for a while holding his eyes open with his fingers.

Things improved when Hannah had the idea of getting them all to tell jokes, and then Sam remembered there was a pack of cards in a drawer in the wall unit. They sat playing cards until six am, when the slow return of light filled them with a sense of triumph. They'd done it. They'd stayed up all night. Sam pulled open the curtains and they watched the sunlight bring the yard back to life. Soon they could make out the trough of flowers, the wheelie bin, the statue of a Greek god Sam's mum had bought from the garden centre and the bricks in the wall that needed pointing.

'I think we should have some coffee now,' Hannah said.

She and Amy went to the kitchen but when they returned Sam couldn't drink all of his as it was so bitter.

If he had drunk the coffee, maybe it wouldn't have happened. But he didn't, and so later on that Saturday afternoon, after lunch, in fact, when there was nothing much on telly and Mum was hoovering in final preparation for the lodger, Sam went up to his room, lay on his bed and shut his eyes. He then had the weirdest dream.

As with all dreams, he thought it was really

happening. First he was in the alternative health centre, Avalon, where his mum worked as a receptionist. He was sitting in the waiting room, staring at a poster of a Sioux chief with piercing blue eyes. There were some other patients in there: two old people, a large German shepherd dog and a man in a brown suit.

The next thing Sam knew, he was back in his bedroom and the second scene of the dream began. 'Your mum has just popped out to get some sugar from Africa,' a policeman said. Sam was not surprised – she had friends in the Serengeti desert. He looked over to his bedroom door but the usual Man City poster had gone, and slowly the door opened. He was curious to see who it would be. It was the man in the brown suit, of course. He was wearing brown shoes with a cut-away design around the toes. His shirt was cream-coloured and his tie had a crest on it, like a coat of arms, with a snake entwined round a harp. The snake wriggled among the strings of the harp, as if it was trying to get out. Sam's eyes moved up to the man's face. He needed a shave – the cleft in his chin looked like a dark ravine. The whole of his face was shadowy because of his hat, a brown hat, the sort Sam had seen men wear in old detective films.

Then it was the third scene of the dream. It wasn't the man in the brown suit who was in Sam's room but Miss Price, the music teacher and deputy head at Park Place. 'You must raise your voices and sing "Hallelujah",' she said. Sam tried, but no sound would come out of his mouth. He tried harder. There was only a soft, raspy squawk. He knew if he couldn't sing Miss Price would send him to the snake pit. Panic gripped him and he forced his mouth open. He heard himself moaning and slowly realised that he really was moaning, curled up on top of his bed, and that he had been asleep.

He was wide awake then. It was still light, so he must have been asleep in the middle of the day.

The dream had left him with a funny feeling. It hadn't exactly been a nightmare, but it hadn't been pleasant either. Perhaps it was what you might call a daymare, Sam thought, and was pleased with himself for making up the word. This daymare had made the normal parts of his life – his mum, his school – seem not normal and even menacing in some way. He felt groggy, his mouth was sticky and he was extremely glad to be awake now.

To help him wake up further he tried to focus on his real day. Mum had been hoovering and now she had stopped. The football might have started already. Mum had said that if the lodger worked out, there'd be extra money and maybe, just maybe, she could buy a second-hand computer. Sometimes they sold them off cheaply at work.

The lodger was coming this afternoon. He was a friend of one of Mum's friends, Shirley, who had recently had twins. You couldn't tell the twins apart. Shirley massaged people's feet at Avalon. She was teaching Sam's mum a little bit about it. Sam wished she had stuck to teaching foot massage rather than mentioning this lodger. He and his mum had been quite happy by themselves and didn't need another person in their house. But, on the other hand, Sam did understand about the extra money coming in. And it seemed that this lodger was desperate for a room – he was starting work at the centre on Monday.

Then Sam remembered that Dean had said to meet him in the Gardens to practise penalties and there was just enough time to have a wash, grab a bite to eat (a jam and peanut butter sandwich) and get out there. All of a sudden he was completely awake. It was as if the dream had never happened. He leapt off the bed and started to get ready.

Halfway down the stairs he heard voices, which he guessed were coming from the kitchen.

One was his mum's, soft-toned, pronouncing each word slowly as if she'd thought about it and meant it, and the other was male, not a local accent, rather posh for round here, Sam thought. He wondered for a moment who it could be.

Of course. The lodger. He felt a bit nervous. You could never tell with adults how they were going to turn out. He had to go into the kitchen if he was going to get that sandwich, and he couldn't avoid the lodger for ever. Resolutely he pushed the door open and there was Mum sitting at the little table, cradling a cup of camomile tea in her hands and smiling up at Sam, with an expression which read, I hope you like him. There too was the back of a man in a brown suit.

'This is Sam,' said his mother.

The man got up and turned round. Sam felt unaccountably shy and looked down. The lodger's shoes were brown with a cut-away design around the toes. His shirt was cream and on his tie was a crest. He needed a shave, and the cleft in his chin was a dark gash. His glasses had tinted blue lenses.

'Hello, Sam,' he said. 'I'm pleased to meet you. I expect we'll get to know each other very well.'

Sam felt his heart thudding in his chest. He shot a look at his mother, but she didn't seem to think anything was strange.

'This is our lodger, Mr Hunter,' she explained.

'Call me Dolf,' he said.

'Mr Hunter – Dolf,' his mother continued, 'has moved up here from London. He's a hypnotherapist, Sam. I'll explain to you another time what that is. He's joining us at Avalon to replace the Reiki master.'

His mum said other stuff too, but Sam wasn't listening. Instead he told himself that this really was his kitchen and he wasn't dreaming. The biscuit tin saying 'Greetings from Scarborough' that Grandma had bought them was sitting on the kitchen table. The clock on the microwave winked at him reassuringly from the corner. A stack of dishes sat by the sink absolutely as usual. There was the calendar with a picture of Chinese mountains donated to them by Amy's parents, advertising the Happy Valley Takeaway. Everything was in its place and as it should be. But there was no escaping it: the lodger had arrived in the kitchen from Sam's own dream.

'I've asked Mr . . . Dolf if he'll eat with us and he said he might occasionally, but he's out a lot of the time. Sam, come and sit down. Don't stand there gawping.'

''S all right,' Sam muttered. 'I was on my way out.'

'Anywhere special?' asked the lodger.

His voice sounded flat, like someone speaking on the radio. It made Sam shudder.

'Just out,' he said, finding himself unwilling to give away any personal information.

'Do you go to school round here?' he asked.

'Park Place,' Sam's mother interjected. Usually Sam disliked his mother's habit of answering for him but now he was grateful. He wanted as little to do with the lodger as possible. 'He's in the first year,' she continued.

'Year 7,' said the lodger, smiling at Sam.

Sam stole a glance at him again. The lodger didn't look so odd any more. The blue lenses of his glasses were spooky, but maybe they were the fashion in London. Lots of men wore brown suits and just as many had stubble on their chins. Also, people did not step out of your dreams and into your life. This lodger, Mr Hunter, was as real and solid and normal as it was possible to be. Sam found his breathing steadying again.

'Make sure you're in before it gets dark,' his mother said.

Just then there was a familiar noise, like a large letter coming through the letter box. Except it wasn't a large letter, but Phoebe, their cat, wriggling in through the cat flap. Once inside the kitchen she stood alert, looking at them, sniffing the air. Then suddenly and quite unexpectedly she bared her teeth and hissed.

'Oh dear!' said Sam's mum. 'I wonder what's upsetting her?'

In an instant the cat made for the cat flap and was out of the house.

'I'd better go too,' Sam said, then turned and ran.

He had to find Hannah and the others as soon as possible.

Chapter Two

Forgetting to look both ways, Sam ran across the road and came to a halt in the Gardens. This was a patch of grass with a playground for the kids and some benches for grown-ups. He and Dean kicked a ball around there sometimes, if no one was around to remind them they shouldn't. Dean was already there, rocking himself to and fro on one of the swings. For a moment he looked much younger than his eleven years. As soon as he saw Sam he scrambled off the swing.

'Did you bring the ball?' he asked.

'No,' Sam said. 'I forgot, but I don't want to play footie now. Something weird has happened. I've got to tell you and the others about it.'

Dean happily fell in with Sam and together they made their way to Hannah's. She lived on the other side of the Gardens in a large house that had been made from two terraced houses joined together. Sam liked it there because the floors didn't join properly and there were two sets of stairs. It was always untidy, which meant you could make as much mess as you liked. He banged on the front door and his luck was in. Hannah confronted them.

'I've got to speak to you,' he said.

Hannah wiped some crumbs from her mouth. She'd been at the biscuit tin.

'Oh, all right. Come in,' she said.

They both followed her into the huge combined kitchen and living room with its television corner. Hannah turned the set off and bounced onto the settee, which was covered by a large red throw. Sam went to join her. It was an old settee and he could feel the springs beneath cutting into him. Dean meanwhile dragged over a beanbag and threw himself onto that, his legs deliberately sticking up in the air.

'So what do you want?' she asked.

'You're going to think I'm mad,' Sam said.

'I already do.'

'I fell asleep this afternoon and I had a weird dream. There was this man in it, a man in a brown suit. And then, when I woke up and went downstairs, there he was. I mean the man in the brown suit was the lodger.'

'Let me get this straight. You dreamed about a man in a brown suit and then you saw one.'

Sam nodded. It was such a relief to tell Hannah. It was a relief, too, to be in her house, with its smells of spicy cooking and sets of exercise books on the table. There were newspapers all over the floor and a *Simpsons* video on the TV. It felt wonderfully normal and safe.

'And you both came over here just to tell me *that*! Sam Williams, you – are – nuts!'

'He's always been completely bonkers,' Dean added.

His friends' scorn was welcome, as it made Sam less scared, but he was angry that they didn't believe he was *right* to have been scared.

'It was the same *man* as in my dream – it wasn't just the brown suit. Nearly every detail was the same, except for the hat. And Phoebe hissed at him.'

Hannah shook her head in a way she must have copied from Mrs Bradshaw, the science teacher at Park Place, who also happened to be her mum. 'Sam, Sam, Sam! Do you know what a dream is?'

Sam wouldn't answer such a patronising question.

'When you go to sleep, your brain sorts out memories of the day, or things you've heard, and so they all pop back into your mind. Everyone dreams, but we only remember our dreams when we sleep lightly. You slept lightly as it was an afternoon sleep, and the man in the brown suit came from Amy's ghost story.'

'Well, how do you explain the fact that the lodger is the same as the man in my dream?' Sam demanded.

'Coincidence,' Hannah said.

'No, it's not,' said Dean. 'I bet he's a spy.'

Both Hannah and Sam ignored him. They were shaping up for a good argument and he was distracting them.

'I believe in dreams,' Sam said. 'Because why would they feel so real if they weren't real?'

'It's your brain chemistry,' Hannah said.

'Go on, then. Explain it. Explain the brain chemistry,' Sam challenged her.

'Well, I will be able to in ten years' time. But I just know, right? I know dreams are your brain playing tricks.'

Hannah looked annoyed, so Sam knew he'd won. But he didn't want to press home his advantage.

'Anyway, I don't like the lodger. He

spooks me.'

'That's because you see him as a threat to your relationship with your mum,' Hannah stated. It was a cruel comment, and she made it, Sam knew, to get her own back.

'No,' Sam said. 'That's not it. There's something not right about him. Phoebe came in and saw him and bared her teeth and hissed.'

'Maybe he's a dog?' suggested Dean, who was now taking his shoes and socks off.

'The cat was surprised to see a stranger,' Hannah said.

'Phoebe likes strangers usually. She jumps on their laps and asks to be stroked.'

'You'll never be able to convince me the whole thing was anything except a coincidence!' Hannah concluded.

Sam wondered why it was they were ever friends. She could be so annoying sometimes, so bossy and insistent she was right. He had to remind himself of the other times, like when he found her crying on the way home from school because the girls had been calling her names, and how she stuck by him while his Grandma was ill, and the fun they had playing on her computer.

'I think we should stalk him,' Dean said suddenly.

Hannah and Sam looked at him.

'Stalk him, like in a film. Keep an eye on him. Follow him and see where he goes. We could keep a notebook of what he does and information about him, and then give it to the police.'

Dean often went into make-believe mode, but something about what he said appealed to Sam. It appealed to Hannah too.

'I've got some notebooks upstairs,' she said. 'We should do it properly. Keep a file on him.'

'If I tell you what I find out—' Sam said.

'I'll give you a special notebook,' Hannah interrupted.

'I've got a camera!' Dean announced. 'I could pretend I was taking a picture of the street and put him in it.'

'Because the truth is, we don't know anything about him,' Hannah added excitedly. 'And he could turn out to be a criminal or something. We have to compile a dossier and get all the facts at our fingertips!'

Dean was now spread-eagled on the beanbag, pretending to gun the others down.

'We must let Amy in on this,' Hannah continued. 'After all, she invented him first.'

'He's *my* lodger!' Sam reminded her.

'He belongs to all of us now,' Hannah said.

The first thing Sam learned was that spying wasn't as much fun as it seemed on TV. He sat on his bed, his ear against the wall, listening for any sounds from the lodger's room that might give his game away. Nothing. Just the occasional murmur of voices on the radio and some music he didn't recognise. Once he collided with the lodger on his way to the bathroom. The lodger was wearing a maroon dressing gown tied by a gold cord and carrying a black washbag. Sam noted that down, but didn't think it would be very useful.

All of Sunday the lodger – or Dolf, as Sam's mum insisted on calling him – occupied himself by moving in. He went out in his car – a beige Citroën Xsara, Sam wrote down – and came back with small household items of no interest. But Sam listed them anyway: an iron, a glass jug you made coffee in, plates, mugs and glasses and some plastic containers. In the late afternoon Sam met up with Hannah, Amy and Dean, and reported back his meagre findings. None of them was impressed. Sam suggested that if they weren't satisfied, *they* should do the trailing. They agreed eagerly, and decided they should all go to Avalon straight after school the next day and find out what they could.

When Sam got home, the lodger was in the kitchen again, chatting with his mum. He looked more normal, in jeans and a black sweatshirt. His mum was giggling a little, which was fairly typical. She had never behaved quite like other people's mothers. It wasn't that she was a widow – a lot of the kids Sam knew had only one parent for one reason or another. It was more that she had never quite settled down. She was always trying new things. Last year she'd started to learn Italian. Three months ago she'd taken up martial arts. Last month she dyed part of her hair pink. Sam couldn't decide whether she just got bored easily or was looking for the thing that would change her life. But he didn't care. She was much more fun than other people's mothers, and she'd be all right as long as she had him around to protect her.

She seemed to be enjoying chatting to the lodger. She grinned even more when she saw Sam.

'Later,' she said to the lodger, then, 'Are you ready for tea, Sam?'

He nodded, staring at the lodger, who avoided eye contact with him and just gazed around the kitchen. Sam didn't like that. Maybe the man was embarrassed, but maybe not. Maybe he knew Sam was on his trail.

'You two ought to get to know each other,' Sam's mum said, and laughed to fill up the gap at the end of her sentence.

'Where have you been, Sam?' asked the lodger, in a friendly enough manner.

'Nowhere,' Sam replied.

'School tomorrow?' he went on.

Sam nodded, desperate to get away. He was saved by the fact the lodger made his apologies and went up to his room instead. Sam decided to note all of that down, including the fact that the lodger's voice sounded strange to his ears – it was hard to say what it was exactly, except that it had a kind of echo. Like the way a voice sounded when it was speaking to you on a telephone in an empty room. That was it. His voice was hollow.

Later that night Dolf Hunter went out. Sam heard him come in and looked at his clock. Eleven pm. He heard going-to-bed noises and then the murmur of the radio. The next thing he knew it was the morning.

Sam was surprised at that. He wasn't usually such a heavy sleeper. His mum had told him that when he was a baby he would stay awake half the night, happy just to lie there in his cot and play. Now he still didn't sleep a lot. Sometimes he wouldn't fall asleep until after twelve, or would wake up in the night and listen to the night sounds, the familiar creaks, the gurgle of pipes and the distant throb of traffic from the town. He also dreamed. He had a sort of recurring dream. There was a forest, a forest he knew very well, that he revisited. It was where a lot of his dreams took place. Different things happened, but it was always the same forest. And in the forest he was always on the verge of discovering something very, very important. But not that night. That night he had slept the sleep of the dead.

School passed in a blur of assembly and lessons and a mad rush to get to the front of the dinner queue. When the final bell went, he met Hannah, Amy and Dean at the school gates. They got on the bus that would take them to the centre of town and climbed up to the top.

'What we ought to do,' Hannah said, 'is interview the other people in your mum's health centre about him. Compile our evidence.'

'You can't do that!' Sam said.

'I can if I'm subtle,' Hannah said.

'I'm going to climb up the drainpipe and peer in through his window, and he'll be using this radio transmitter to send messages to Mexico,' Dean interjected.

'Why Mexico?' Hannah was annoyed. 'We're not at war with Mexico! Why would you want to send secret messages to Mexico? It's part of the United States . . . I think.'

Amy said, 'He came into our takeaway last night.'

They were all quiet. 'He bought prawns in oyster sauce with fried rice. I took his money. He asked me what my name was and whether I knew Sam. Then he gave me a present.'

Sam and the others were stunned.

'A present?'

Amy reached into her blazer pocket and her clenched fist emerged. Slowly she opened it to reveal a small doll, no bigger than a thumb, made of coloured straw, red, black and yellow. Its eyes were two tiny black dots.

'This,' she said.

'A doll! You're rather young to be given a doll,' Hannah remarked.

'Let's have it!' Dean grabbed the doll from her and held it to his ear. 'I can hear radio signals!'

Amy snatched it back from him, her eyes blazing. 'It's *mine*!' she shouted.

Some old ladies behind them tut-tutted.

Just as Sam had expected, going to Avalon was a bit of an anticlimax. They were spotted immediately by Leo who gave Indian head massage. Even though they could see Sam's mum at the reception desk, Leo told them to wait upstairs in his room, out of everybody's way. They sat there for a few minutes until Hannah suddenly got up.

'Come with me, Sam. I'm going to ask some questions!'

Sam followed her down to reception.

'Only a few more minutes,' his mum said. 'It's nice of you to come and meet me.'

'Mrs Williams,' Hannah said, sounding like one of those political interviewers on TV, 'can you explain exactly what hypnotherapy is?'

'Yes, Hannah. If you have a phobia – say you're scared of heights – or maybe you want help giving up smoking, or you want more confidence, you can go to a hypnotherapist. He puts you in a state of deep relaxation and can send messages to your subconscious to help you overcome your fears or your craving for cigarettes.'

'Does it work?'

'A lot of people think so. You see, your subconscious mind is a lot more powerful than your conscious mind.'

'What do you have to do to become a hypnotherapist?'

'You study and take diplomas, I think. And it helps to have a natural ability, the knack of making people relax. I'd be no good!' Sam's mum laughed.

Hannah picked up a leaflet. 'Mr A. Hunter – hypnotherapist. Who's that?'

'That's our new lodger, Hannah. Adolf Hunter. But we call him Dolf.'

'Aah,' exclaimed Hannah. 'I see. Mrs Williams, do you know what he did before he was a hypnotherapist?'

At that moment there were footsteps coming down the stairs and a small, plump lady emerged, with the lodger behind her.

'Thank you,' she murmured. 'I'll be back next week.'

Sam nudged Hannah and she got the message. She stared up at Dolf Hunter. Sam could swear he stared right back at her, and not in a friendly way. Sam's mum introduced them and, realising Hannah could ask no more questions, Sam led her back to the waiting room.

'I saw him!' Hannah announced, jubilant.

The others begged her for details.

'He's really tall, about six foot, with yellowy, piercing eyes. And the way he looked at me, I thought, he doesn't like children.'

'He gave me the doll,' Amy said.

Then they heard voices and were quiet. Dolf Hunter was offering Sam's mum a lift home, but she refused, saying the children had come all the way to meet her. Suddenly Sam was very glad they were there. They ran to the large bay window and watched Dolf get into his car, which was parked in the forecourt of the building. Dean was pretending to gun him down from the window.

'Dean!' said Sam's mum. 'What on earth are you doing?'

The children swivelled round. Sam's mum didn't look too pleased.

'What on earth are you playing at? Now, don't let your games get out of hand. Think if Mr Hunter had seen you. Sam – I would have thought you'd know better. And from now on I want you to make an effort to get on with him. Believe me, he's a very nice man. He can't help it if he's not used to children.'

Later that night Sam's mum suggested that Mr Hunter come down for coffee so they could all three talk. In reality, it was Sam's mum who did most of the talking.

'Sam, I thought you'd be interested to know that Dolf has travelled all over the world, haven't you, Dolf?'

'I have visited many countries,' he admitted, in that flat voice of his.

'He's had so many different jobs. He drove a train in India!'

Sam knew that was said to interest him. Normally he would have been quite glad to make the acquaintance of someone who knew about engines. But not now. More and more, he could sense Dolf's hostility to him. He was fairly certain it wasn't his imagination. Even though Dolf was sitting on the sofa in their lounge, and should have looked at ease, his posture, Sam noticed, was stiff. Dolf was watching him as much as he was watching Dolf. There *was* something strange about him. Sam's gran used to say he had a sixth sense and he had never been quite sure what she meant until now. Everything about the lodger felt *wrong*. Or maybe, like his mum had said, it was just that the game had got out of hand and Sam had convinced himself the lodger was peculiar.

Whichever it was, Dolf Hunter wasn't inclined to talk about his experiences travelling the world. Instead he seemed content to let Sam's mum talk for both of them.

'Dolf's been able to travel so much,' she continued, 'because he doesn't have any family – at least in this country. That's right, isn't it, Dolf? Never mind,' she said, addressing her comment to him. 'You're welcome to muck in with us. Isn't he, Sam?'

Sam saw that Dolf was flexing his fingers as if he was slowly massaging the air. It was a strange movement. And then his eyes turned to Sam's. Sam wanted to look away, but found he couldn't. For one awful moment their gaze was locked. Only when Dolf turned his head was Sam free. Sam felt his heart pounding. He glanced at his mother to see if she had noticed anything, but she was oblivious.

'Oh, you men!' Sam's mother continued. 'I'm having to make all the conversation! Dolf, you said you had some photographs of the ashram you stayed in, in India. Can we see those?'

'I'm afraid I left them upstairs on my bed,' he said.

'I'll get them,' Sam volunteered, and quick as a flash he was out of the room and flying up the stairs.

It was a relief to be out of the kitchen, but also here was an opportunity to get a glimpse of

Dolf's room. Hannah, Amy and Dean would be seriously impressed, although by now Sam was almost hoping he wouldn't find anything, because Dolf was beginning to spook him. If he came across the evidence to suggest that *he* was the one who was being over-imaginative, secretly he would be glad.

He opened Dolf's door. The first thing he noticed was that it was cold, much colder than the rest of the house. Perhaps he'd turned off the radiator. There were the photos, on the bed, in a yellow Supasnaps wallet. But first Sam looked around him. The room was sparsely furnished. There was a dresser where the pots and pans were. A table, with a laptop on it. A TV. A chair, with his brown suit hung over it, and a brown hat on the seat. Sam began to tremble. It was the same brown hat from his daymare, the hat with the brim that shaded Dolf's face and made him look like a detective.

It was the hat that did it. It made Sam absolutely certain that all his suspicions were right. Or rather that Dolf Hunter was all wrong, all wrong and dangerous. So even more reason for finding out as much about him as he possibly could. Again his eyes searched the room. He saw that on the bedside table was a small radio and a book in a language he didn't recognise. Under the bed were the pair of brown shoes and a small red bowl. Sam pulled it out. In it were some small dolls, the same as he had given Amy. He took out a few, then heard someone running up the stairs. Fear and embarrassment swept through him. In his confusion he remembered to pick up the photos but still had tight hold of the dolls. He kicked the bowl back under the bed. Dolf appeared at the door.

'I thought you were having trouble finding them,' he said.

For a moment Sam could have sworn that

the lodger's eyes looked yellow. Or was it a trick of the light? Only this time Sam did not feel compelled to meet his gaze.

'No. Here they are.' Sam noticed his voice sounded thin and young. He offered the photos to Dolf and both of them returned downstairs.

Sam kept tight hold of the dolls. While his mum and Dolf were looking at the photos he managed to get them into his jeans pocket. Once he'd done that, he relaxed and pretended to look at the photos.

Meanwhile his mind was racing. What on earth was a grown man without children doing with miniature dolls? Were they something to do with hypnotherapy? Why had he given one to Amy? He wondered whether he should have a word with his mum, but he knew she would either laugh at him or tell him off for snooping round the lodger's room. The best thing to do, he decided, was to see Hannah, Dean and Amy first thing in the morning.

As soon as he could, he excused himself, pleading tiredness. Back in his bedroom, he took the dolls out of his pocket and examined them again. He'd taken three of them. They were identical except for small variations in the straw. He hoped Dolf wouldn't notice they were gone. He had to have them, because they were evidence. Evidence of what, he couldn't work out yet. He would consult Hannah – she was the brains of the outfit.

Sam swiftly got ready for bed, dashed into the shared bathroom and brushed his teeth, listening all the time for the lodger. But he had not returned upstairs. Now Sam allowed himself to feel uneasy that he had left his mother alone with Dolf. Maybe he would have a word with her in the morning – he'd decide later. He went back to his bedroom and wished for the first time in his life that he had a lock on his door. So that Dolf would not find the dolls, he put them under his pillow.

He didn't fall asleep for ages. He waited until Dolf had settled in his room and even until his radio had become silent. It was well after midnight. Still Sam lay awake. The sensible bit of his brain tried to tell him he was imagining things. Dolf Hunter was just awkward and shy, an everyday, ordinary man. Then a wave of fear would surge through him and Sam knew, just knew, that he and his mum were in danger.

But the funny thing about fear is that it comes and goes. In a space between the waves of fear, Sam started thinking about school, and whether he'd have much homework over the weekend. The thought of homework made him sleepy. He could stay awake no longer, and it was then that a most extraordinary thing happened.

Chapter Three

Sam was dreaming. He knew he was dreaming because he was in his forest. In fact he was sitting on a large, mossy, toppled log, his feet just a little way above the ground. It was his forest, all right. He was in the same clearing where his dreams always seemed to begin and there was the stone with a freshly painted target on it in green and gold. He called it the Shooting Stone.

Only something was different. It all seemed so much more vivid. The colours, for one thing. He looked closely at his Shooting Stone. Its green concentric circles were bright lime green, and the gold glittered like the very precious metal it came from. The leaves on the ground were many different colours – red, blue, chocolaty brown, gold, silver, deep violet. Sam himself felt more *awake* than he had ever been in his dreams.

Normally when he was in the forest things just happened to him, as if he had no control. Now his veins seemed to buzz and filled his legs with an unusual strength. He knew he was dreaming, but at the same time he felt more alive than he could remember. Then with embarrassment he realised that he was wearing his school blazer, his pyjama bottoms and his old trainers, the ones Mum threw out ages ago. So it must be a dream after all.

Sam smiled to himself. He decided that in a moment he would leave the log and investigate the forest. In all his previous dreams, he was moved along in the direction the dream took. Now he was free to make his own plans. He reached down and picked up a handful of old leaves. As he did, they disintegrated into fine confetti that sprinkled the ground. They gave off musical notes, like tiny bells ringing. Sam repeated his action, pleased with his discovery. Then he got up. He picked up a stone – a round, smooth pebble – and hurled it at the

Shooting Stone. It slammed into the centre of the target and there was applause from the nearby trees. Sam looked up into the branches and there, as he had expected, were the greenbirds. The applause was their song and came from the vibration of their wooden beaks. Sam was glad to see them. He knew they were his friends.

Time to explore. Picking up a bough that had fallen from a nearby birch, he moved off into the forest, his legs light and full of vigour. Sunbeams trickled through the branches and gave a bluish tinge to the thickly wooded area. The trees were packed more and more closely, but he was not afraid. In fact, the more dense the woodland, the safer he felt. Like old and trusted friends, the trees nudged him, reminding him they were there, that they were on his side. One nimbly removed his roots from the path so Sam would not trip. Two other trees kicked a football around, and as Sam reached them, he headed the ball right up into the tree tops, where more greenbirds applauded.

Soon the trees thinned out and Sam was glad to see he had reached the river, where many of his dreams had taken place in the past. There was the small jetty with its uneven planks of wood. There was the raft, stocked with provisions: bottles of cola, crisps and scrambled eggs. His mother was on the other side of the river, giving Indian head massage to Mr Pearson, the head of Park Place Community School, and the head was actually wearing an Indian headdress, which suited him. He had also grown a beard.

Sam felt his chin and discovered that he had grown a beard too. Not wanting one, he pulled it off. His mother had gone now and he had the river to himself. He removed his trainers and splashed his feet in the water. It was warm, like a bath. But the air was cool and fresh and filled Sam with inexplicable happiness. He kicked more and more strongly until silver droplets of water were raining everywhere.

Then he thought he could hear more splashing, not just the splashing he was making but something different. He was suddenly still and listened very carefully. There was a slow splashing sound, as if a boat was coming down the river. He was afraid. The sky above him darkened. Usually in his dreams he was the centre of all the action. Things happened to him, he was there in the middle of every scene. The fact that someone else had been doing something separate from him in his Dream Kingdom was very disturbing. He found himself shrivelling and now he was very, very small, no more than half a metre.

His first thought was to hide. He crept among the reeds by the side of the jetty and waited. He then realised that his new size was an advantage since he could spy on whoever was coming down the river. It grew darker and darker. The only light was from the occasional flash of a glow-worm. Sam saw a dark shadow move slowly along the water. It was a long, black barge, oozing a multicoloured slime that transformed into snakes. The snakes set themselves alight and, as they did so, formed laser beams that zigzagged along the river bank, searching for something. Sam knew they were looking for him. He wished he were smaller. As if by magic, he discovered that he was.

A beam of light flung itself down by his side. Then another one landed at his other side. After what seemed an age, he saw another beam flash further along the river bank. He had not been found. He was safe. Now he was growing again, the sky lightened and the threat had passed. A greenbird flew down with a newspaper cutting in his beak which announced that City had beaten United again.

Now there was another sound but this one was not threatening. It was the clack-clack-clack of an antique helicopter, made in 1523 by a famous Roman professor. It was constructed of a rich mahogany and its rotor blades were ebony. It landed on the opposite side of the river and Amy got out.

'Where am I?' she asked.

Sam leapt across to join her.

'In my forest,' he said.

'I usually go to the moon,' she said, looking confused.

Sam shrugged. 'Welcome to my forest,' he said.

Some greenbirds flew to her with red liquorice laces in their beaks and Amy took them, weaving a necklace for herself.

'Can you fly?' she asked Sam.

Sam tried flapping his arms but nothing happened. 'I don't think so. But look!' He leapt into the air as if he was saving a goal. He shot up more than a metre off the ground. 'I can do that,' he said.

'But you came down. I don't come down.' Amy gave a small jump, waggled her ankles, fell slowly on to her stomach and began swimming in the air, a sort of doggy paddle. She circled Sam, laughing.

'I love doing this,' she said. 'But it's nothing. I can go higher and higher. Watch.'

As if she was surfacing from a dive, Amy shot up through the air until she was beyond the tree tops. She seemed to float on the currents of air. Sam desperately wanted to be there with her. Amy swooped down again.

'It's easy,' she said. 'Copy me.'

Sam did. He waggled his ankles, jumped and dived into the air. It worked. He was afloat. He tried a breaststroke first, but he only inched forward very slowly. So he changed to an overarm crawl. Now he moved more quickly through the air, gaining confidence all the time.

'Amazing!' he called out to Amy.

'Follow me!' she called from a couple of metres above him.

Sam did so, but found it hard to keep up with Amy, who was used to flying. Gradually she took him higher and higher. The higher they got, the easier it seemed to be to fly. Sam felt himself floating on cushions of air and needed only the smallest arm movements or the kick of his feet as rudders to move wherever he wanted. Then he looked below him.

'This is my kingdom, Amy,' he said.

Spread out like that, bathed in golden sunlight, it was beautiful. Sam could see the clearing where his dream had started, and the blue forest. There was the main road through the wood that led to the deserted cottage. Bears had lived there once. Grazing in the meadows was a herd of deer, tiny from this perspective. There was the small hill with its pagoda and brass band. He could also see the orange wood, the spice tree thicket and the carousel. Everything he had ever dreamed was there, his own kingdom. He circled above it all like an eagle.

Thinking back to what had happened earlier, he searched the land for signs of the black barge, but there were none.

'Amy,' he asked, 'when you were coming here, did you see anything? Did you see a plastic trumpet with wheels?'

That was strange. It was not what Sam had meant to say. He had meant to ask her about the barge. He tried again.

'Amy, when you were in your helicopter, did you see a watering can?'

No, not a watering can.

'Did you see George Washington with a kangaroo?'

It was impossible. The words would not come.

Amy said, 'I want to go back to the moon. You can come with me if you like.'

She took off like a rocket, burning a path

through the darkening sky. She was too fast. Sam could not follow. Without her by his side, he found himself drifting slowly to the ground.

He wasn't surprised when he woke up in his bed. It was seven fifteen in the morning. He had just had the most vivid dream of his whole life. Even now he could remember every detail, and he lay in bed, recalling it all – the clearing, the greenbirds, the Shooting Stone, the river, the jetty, Amy's arrival, their flight, her vanishing into the sky. He remembered everything. Even his mother's guest appearance and the head of Park Place in an Indian headdress. He smiled at the memory and knew he'd laugh again when he saw him in school.

He heard noises in the bathroom and realised that the lodger had got there before him. But it didn't matter. His dream had dissipated the fear he had felt last night. He stared at the ceiling and decided that he'd tell Amy the part she had played in his dream. It was weird when you dreamed about your friends. It made you feel kind of closer to them. And then he remembered. It wasn't just the dream he had to report back on, he had to tell his mates about last night and how he was nearly caught red-handed by the lodger. He leapt out of bed, raring to go.

Sam didn't see Amy and Hannah until break, because they were in different classes. He and Dean made their way through the knots of other kids in the playground and around the back of the annex. Amy was with Hannah and they were sharing their food. That happened every break. Hannah's mum packed her a healthy snack of apples and bananas while Amy was given crisps and biscuits. Amy ate Hannah's and Hannah ate Amy's.

'Hi, you two,' Hannah greeted them. 'Any developments with you-know-who?'

Sam nodded mysteriously.

'Go on, then,' Hannah demanded.

Sam related all that had happened yesterday night. Finally, with a flourish, he brought the dolls out of his pocket.

'And here they are,' he said. 'The same sort as he gave Amy.'

'Let me see them,' Hannah said. She took them carefully from Sam and examined them closely. 'Maybe he makes and sells them. Or uses them in his hypnotherapy. Or maybe in his spare time he has a craft stall.'

'No,' said Dean. 'If you took them apart, you'd find a stolen diamond in each. I bet you would. Can we try it?'

'We'd better not,' Sam shouted at him. 'Just in case Dolf wants them back.'

'What did you say?' Dean shouted in reply.

The playground was noisy. Not only were there kids yelling, but there was also an excavator nearby digging up the ground for a new school extension. Sam had to shout even louder to make Amy hear him.

'I had a dream about you last night!'

'I had a dream about you!' Amy shouted back.

That interested Sam. Luckily at that moment the excavator stopped. He drew Amy to one side.

'In my dream you arrived in a helicopter by my river.'

Amy stared at him, her eyes wide as saucers. 'A wooden helicopter, made by the Romans.'

'You said you usually go to the moon.'

'I do,' she said. 'And then I took you flying.'

'We saw my kingdom—'

'The cottage and the deer – tiny deer—'

'You vanished—'

'I went back to the moon—'

'What are you two gabbing on about?' Hannah interrupted.

The dolls were clasped tightly in her hand and Sam noticed that her knuckles were white.

'Hannah, this is really strange. Mega-strange. Amy and I have had the same dream.'

'We have,' Amy confirmed.

Slowly Sam and Amy told the other two exactly what had happened to them. Dean tried to listen, but as usual his mind wandered. The teachers said he had some attention disorder thing, but Sam knew it was just Dean's way. Hannah looked unimpressed.

'It's another coincidence,' she said stubbornly.

'But the *details* were the same!' Sam shouted at her.

'I know,' Dean cried. 'The dolls are poisoned and he kills rats with them. No – I know. The dolls make you go into somebody else's dreams.'

'Don't be so stup—' Hannah began, but

Sam shut her up by covering her mouth with his hand. He asked Dean to repeat what he'd said.

'The dolls make you go into somebody else's dream.'

'Amy,' said Sam, 'where did you put your doll last night?'

'Under my pillow,' she replied.

'So did I,' Sam said.

'I want one,' said Dean. 'Then I can visit you.'

'Stop it, all of you! Don't be so babyish,' Hannah shouted.

Sam ignored her. 'I know! Let's try an experiment. Let's each take a doll and each sleep with it under our pillow tonight. If we all meet up in a dream, then this is real. This is really happening. And it's got something to do with the lodger. And we've got to keep it to ourselves, because no one else would ever believe us. Not in a million million years.'

'Sleep with a *doll* under my pillow!' snorted Hannah. 'Like, how young do you think I am?'

'If you don't,' said Sam, with all the authority he could muster, 'then you're out of this. We investigate the lodger on our own.'

Sam was eye to eye with Hannah, only she didn't look defiant, as he had expected. She was terrified and silently pleading with him to drop the whole thing. What had changed her? Without saying anything, she handed him back the dolls.

He took them from her. They felt warm, very warm, as if they had been in the sun. They seemed to give off a vibration and in fact, when Sam examined them, they were blurred, almost as if they were moving faster than his eye could see.

He knew that Hannah believed him now.

Chapter Four

School seemed to drag even more than usual. All Sam wanted was to get through the day, arrive home, eat and go to bed as soon as possible. It was vital they experiment properly and discover whether the dolls really did let you into other people's dreams. Sam's doll was in his trouser pocket now, and every so often he checked it was still there, felt the tiny ridges of straw with his fingertips and wondered.

Afternoon registration was twice as long as it should have been. There was a special message from the head about uniforms. Apparently regulations had been infringed and there was to be a general tightening up. All shirts were to be tucked in on school premises, girls' skirts had to be a certain length, no jewellery, that sort of thing. And all school blazers had to be bought from

Bagthorpe and Collier's Outfitters and all black sweatshirts had to have the school crest on them. There was a letter to take home about it. Sam turned his into a paper aeroplane and aimed it at Dean. Unfortunately it hit one of the girls in the back row, Katie and Lauren and Emma and Claire.

'Watch it!' one of them said. Sam wasn't sure which. He always thought about these girls as a single entity. They were rarely apart. Sam didn't care for them much. Since they'd turned twelve they looked down on everyone else in the class, making out they were much older. Recently they'd all begun to wear the same shade of lip gloss and hitch up their skirts.

'Miss! Miss!' whined Katie and Lauren and Emma and Claire. 'Sam Williams is throwing paper aeroplanes!'

'Well, stop it, Sam,' the teacher said, but she didn't seem bothered. She was so busy with paperwork, Sam reckoned, she'd quite like to turn all her lists and letters and notices into paper aeroplanes and throw them at the Head.

At the end of the day he walked home with Hannah, Amy and Dean. Dean was fizzing with excitement and Hannah had turned scientific again.

'I'm not saying that I think it will work, just that it's an intriguing experiment. In the interests of biochemistry. We could all be suffering from a mass delusion, you know.'

No one was really listening to her. They approached the parade of shops opposite the Gardens, where Amy's takeaway was. The shop on the corner had recently been sold and now workmen were busy renovating it.

'What's that going to be?' Dean asked anyone who was listening.

'A new BurgerWorld,' Amy said.

'Yesss!' Dean punched the air. 'A Burger World Big One with Turbo Fries!'

'Actually, my parents aren't very pleased,' Amy said. 'It might take business away from us.'

'That's a point,' Hannah said. 'But different sort of people eat burgers and Chinese food. And you can eat in at BurgerWorld. Or you could get a milkshake at BurgerWorld and a meal at your place.'

Sam privately thought that Hannah would. She seemed to get a lot of comfort from food. For all her bossiness and know-it-all-ness, Sam was certain that Hannah was unhappy. Even though she was one of the cleverest kids in the school, she was never satisfied with her marks, always striving to be that bit better. Sam preferred to take life more easily. Getting by was good enough for him.

The four of them parted outside the Happy Valley.

'See you in your dreams!' joked Hannah.

Sam lay in bed, eyes wide open. There was no way he was going to be able to get to sleep. His doll was snugly embedded under his pillow, his light was off and his room was dark save for the red digits on his alarm clock. For all he knew, Dean and Amy and Hannah had fallen asleep ages ago and were getting up to all sorts of mischief without him.

Sleep! he commanded himself. No use. He tried counting sheep, but it was too boring and, besides, he got confused at about forty-seven. Then he tried to recall last night's dream, and his forest, and bit by bit he felt himself relax and his limbs get heavy. He snuggled into his favourite position, legs drawn up to his chest, face almost buried in the pillow.

Suddenly every nerve in his body was alert. There was someone in his room. He could feel a pressure on his side. There was a living, breathing being with him, tapping him lightly just below his shoulder. Sam froze. Was it Dolf, coming for the doll? Dare he open his eyes and see?

Something tickled his face. Sam breathed a sight of relief. It was Phoebe's whiskers. The cat had obviously hidden under his bed and, thinking Sam was asleep, had come out to prepare herself for a very comfortable night indeed. Sam scooped her up and put her outside the door.

It was then that he realised that Dolf was coming up the stairs. Sam shot back into his bedroom. He heard the cat give an unearthly howl and head for the kitchen and the cat flap. Sam listened to the lodger prepare for bed. Dolf must have turned on the radio, as he could make out the whine and crackle of distant stations in faraway lands.

Sam thought he'd never get to sleep now. If only it was possible to re-create the moment when drowsiness overtook you, like a thief waiting in ambush, like a kidnapper enfolding you in a black cloak, struggling in its warm, soft clutch . . .

Where are they all? Sam thought.

He was sitting on the log in the clearing. At the other side two greenbirds were playing Patience with a deck of plastic cards. Dean, Hannah and Amy were nowhere to be seen. That didn't worry Sam. He was confident his friends would turn up soon.

From behind an old, crumbling oak tree City's centre forward lobbed him a high ball and he deftly swung it back. He looked up and there was a fleet of paper aeroplanes. He knew it would be easy to get drawn into the pleasures of his own forest and realised that he had to make an effort to find his friends.

'Dean?' he called.

His voice echoed among the trees and came back to him in a shower of softer Dean, Dean, Deans. But no response.

'Hannah?'

Another echo and the laughter of the greenbirds. One of them was performing a crazy breakdance on a bough close by.

'Amy?' Nothing. Silence. But it was a waiting silence. It made Sam certain that Amy was nearby but hiding. He looked up and squinted to see if she was in the trees. He walked over to the Shooting Stone, crunching leaves, to see if she was behind that. Too easy. It was just like Amy to hide this way. He pushed through into the thickly wooded area behind the clearing and listened. Nothing. Yet he was aware of Amy's presence and knew he would find her.

Returning to the clearing, he realised where she was. He approached the log carefully, quietly, and when he got there, bent down and put his face to the hollow interior. As he expected, there, three times larger than life, was Amy's face, grinning from ear to ear. Sam grinned back.

'Come in!' she said. 'There's loads of room.'

Sam wasn't so sure, but saw Amy's face recede into the distance. He crouched down and stuck his face in. The weird thing was, further down, the log's interior was much, much bigger than he would have imagined. He poked his whole head into the log, followed by the top half of his body. It was a tight squeeze. His arms were jammed tight and he was struggling to breathe. He wriggled his way forward, moving each shoulder alternately, making slow progress. There was a sharp, earthy smell mixing with an odour of pine. The bark pressing against his skin was cold and firm.

Then, as if he was being fired from a gun, he shot though into the inner chamber. Amy was there, smiling, delighted.

'Time to go to the moon!' she said.

Naturally there was a rocket in the chamber, sitting comfortably on a launch pad. Sam followed Amy onto it. The control deck was reassuringly familiar. He had seen countless similar ones on TV. Sam was itching to push some buttons, pull some levers and achieve lift-off. However, this proved to be unnecessary. The rocket began to spin like the drum of a washing machine. Sam found himself flung to the sides of the craft, panting for breath.

'Stop!' he managed to cry.

Obligingly, the spacecraft did. Together Sam and Amy opened the door to be bathed in a reddish glow.

'The moon!' Amy shouted with glee. She catapulted out of the craft, kicked her legs and floated easily off into the distance. Here goes, thought Sam, kicking his legs, and heading off in pursuit.

It was odd being in Amy's Dream Kingdom. It felt like visiting somebody else's house, when the people who live there seem completely at home, but to you the chairs and tables look different and in the wrong places, and you have to think carefully about how you're going to behave. Sam was similarly cautious now. He decided just to follow Amy, taking it all in.

The sky glowed red. That was the most noticeable thing about Amy's kingdom. But even though the sky was red, there seemed to be plenty of light, except it congregated in particular places, like spotlights. It was hard to make out the more shadowy areas. As far as Sam could tell, the land was just red dust, dimpled with craters. Stray objects littered the ground. He thought he saw old telephones, a rusty wok, a doll's pram and a mattress with the stuffing coming out. Then Amy strapped a large floodlight to her stomach and the whole of the land beneath was illuminated.

He could see now that a network of pathways connected different parts of the dusty wasteland of Amy's kingdom. In some of the hills he could make out openings like large burrows and in the distance a collection of small houses with shingled roofs.

The ground rose under them and a current of air lifted them. Sam found he was peering down into a valley where a complicated system of conveyor belts carried water along and ladies in bonnets were drawing it off in buckets. There was a delicious smell of sweet and sour sauce.

'That's the Happy Valley,' Amy explained.

They finally landed in one of the brightly lit areas. Sam found himself beside a large lake of navy-blue water, with little wavelets flecked with gold lapping at the shore. Near them was a booth where an elderly Chinese man was handing out ice cream. Sam accepted one with multicoloured hundreds and thousands on top. He tasted it and was delighted to discover that in Amy's kingdom you could eat real food. The ice cream melted in his mouth. It was the best, the creamiest, he had ever eaten in his whole life.

Sam looked out over the lake, which danced and sparkled in the light. Then, in a cascade of water, a dolphin appeared, carrying on its back none other than Dean and Hannah. Amy clapped her hands excitedly. The dolphin cane to the surface smoothly and brought its passengers to the shore. Sam felt a surge of happiness.

'Try the ice cream,' he said. 'It's meltylicious.'

Soon all four of them were enjoying ice creams, seated around a white garden table. Again Sam was surprised at how alive he felt. It was as if the ice cream was giving him the power to think and talk clearly.

'If we remember this in the morning, then the dream dolls have worked,' he said. 'But I don't know what we can do next. Or what we should do next.'

'We can have holidays in each other's Dream Kingdoms,' Amy suggested.

'I like yours better than mine,' Dean announced.

'What about your kingdom, Hannah?' Sam asked.

'I don't have one,' she said.

'But everyone dreams!'

'Not me. Dreams are nonsense.'

Sam felt it was rude to pry further. Your Dream Kingdom was a private land, and other people could go there only by invitation. If Hannah wasn't ready to talk about hers, that was her business. He knew how frightened she was really. It was her other side, being frightened. And who could have guessed that silent, secretive Amy would be so generous as to have them here and let them share her ice cream. Other people might think Amy was reserved, but they were wrong.

'You must all come to my Dream Kingdom!' Sam declared.

'How do you get there?' Dean asked.

'In the rocket,' Sam replied.

'But the rocket has gone,' Amy announced.

That was a problem.

'I know,' said Sam. 'You must all imagine yourselves there!'

As he said that, he began to visualise his own Dream Kingdom. There was his clearing, the log, the greenbirds, the Shooting Stone. His river, the trees. He could feel a soft wind ruffle his hair and heard the gentle footfalls of the deer who lived in the forest. The damp, cool smell of earth surrounded him.

And he was back in his Dream Kingdom. A flurry of leaves descended from the branches announcing his arrival. But he was alone. There were no signs at all of Amy, Hannah or Dean. Immediately Sam realised his mistake, and it was a big one. *He* could imagine his Dream Kingdom, because he knew it so well. Amy had been here only once, and Dean and Hannah, never. So they couldn't imagine it and were unable to follow him. Another time maybe. He would have to put his mind to working out a way of getting them here.

But for now, he thought, he'd take a stroll through his kingdom. It seemed to be late afternoon and the forest was bathed in a golden light. Everything – the trees, the bracken, the small flowers – looked more vivid than usual, but also sad, as if they had lost something. Sam couldn't shake off a feeling of foreboding. All was not as it should be. He made his way towards a large, elderly oak tree. The trunk seemed to sag. The branches drooped. Sap oozed from the bark like tears.

There was something else amiss. His kingdom was silent. The greenbirds had vanished. Their constant twittering was a sign that all was well and now it had gone. Sam hurried back to his clearing, increasingly alarmed.

The clearing looked the same. There was his log, and the surrounding trees seemed normal. If they were in shade it was only because the sun was going down. There was the Shooting Stone. But there was something on it. Slowly he approached. He saw a soft, brown hat, like the ones detectives wore in old films. And a pair of glasses, glasses Sam recognised, ones with blue-tinted lenses. He knew immediately what had happened. Dolf had been here, and without Sam's permission.

It was the most terrible feeling. Dolf had been here, like a thief in the night, leaving his calling card. He *wanted* Sam to know he'd been there. How dare he – how *dare* he violate Sam's Dream Kingdom! Sam filled with anger. But it wasn't just anger that coursed through him, there was fear there too, a crippling, icy fear. And a growing certainty that Dolf had taken away part of himself, had robbed him of something.

He picked up the hat and glasses, then put them down. They felt quite real. But he must have triggered an alarm, because suddenly his head was filled with a deafening ringing. The hat and glasses were booby-trapped.

No, they weren't. The alarm was Sam's bedside alarm. It was seven thirty in the morning, real time. Yet Sam awoke sweating, every muscle in his body tense. Relax, he told himself, it was all a dream. You're back in the boring old real world.

He reassured himself by looking round his bedroom. There was the City poster on the door. There was his school uniform in a heap on the floor. There was the sunlight making the curtains look semi-transparent. There, on his desk, were his football encyclopaedias and last night's homework – and something else. Sam sat up in bed, pulling the duvet tightly around him.

On his desk were a brown hat and a pair of blue-tinted glasses.

Chapter Five

Sam's morning brain was fresh and clear. He was quite certain that the hat and glasses had not been there when he had fallen asleep. So Dolf had put them there, either in his Dream Kingdom or in reality, in the middle of the night. Sam knew he would have to be bold. He scrambled into his clothes, opened his bedroom door and looked around the landing. Dolf's door was wide open and he was elsewhere.

But not in the bathroom. Sam entered, got himself ready, then returned to his bedroom and took the hat and glasses. Carrying them gingerly, as though they might explode at any moment, he took them downstairs. As he did so, he could hear his mother's voice trilling merrily among the clatter of plates and a rush of water from the taps.

'Now that's so interesting! That had never

occurred to me before, Dolf! So you're saying what I need to do is relax for a while, and not try so hard to be different. Do you know, I'd never seen myself as someone who kept trying to make myself stand out from the crowd? When you put it like that, I can see that I might have a problem. But what can I do about it?'

Sam stood by the closed door, still as a stone, clutching the hat and glasses.

'You should try hypnotherapy,' came Dolf's voice. 'I have a free slot at the end of the day. There will be no charge.'

'That's so kind of you, but you must let me do something for you in return. I'll cook you dinner. What's your favourite food?'

'Eggs.'

'Just eggs? Why not a Spanish omelette, with some red and green peppers?'

'No. Plain eggs will do.'

'I expect those years in India have left you

with a delicate stomach. I understand.'

'Thank you,' said Dolf. 'I knew you would. I hope to make you understand many things.'

Sam chose that moment to open the kitchen door with a flourish.

'I found these in my room,' he said, as loudly as he could, offering the hat and glasses to Dolf.

'Now how could they have got there?' Sam's mother questioned.

Sam was wondering exactly the same thing and was waiting to hear Dolf's reply. He glanced at his mother and noticed she was wearing a grey blouse he hadn't seen before and a neat black skirt. She'd tied her shaggy hair back into a ponytail. The next thing he knew, Dolf seized the hat and glasses. Sam let go quickly. He felt a spasm of pain in his head and he sensed that Dolf was alarmed. Had he left his things in Sam's Dream Kingdom by accident? Yet when he spoke, he sounded as calm as ever.

'Does your son sleepwalk?' Dolf addressed Sam's mother.

'Not that I know of,' she replied. 'But there's always a first time.'

'I dare say he went to the bathroom in the night and walked into my room by mistake while I was asleep. Confused, he took my hat and glasses. Thank you for returning them.'

'No!' Sam began, challenging Dolf with furious eyes. But as his eyes locked on Dolf's, he was overcome again with a sort of paralysis. He couldn't wrest his gaze away from the flat, yellowish eyes of his adversary. 'No. I mean, I don't remember. I remember nothing.'

'Then it *does* sound as if he's been sleepwalking!' Sam's mother declared. 'I wonder why? Maybe it's a growth spurt. Or your body isn't tired enough at night, Sam.'

Sam tried to unfix his gaze from Dolf's, but it was proving impossible. And while Dolf held him, the only words he found in his head were, *I remember nothing*. Perhaps it was true. He remembered nothing. Except for one thing from his dream the night before, Amy's ice cream, and the way the hundreds and thousands danced and sparkled on its surface, like tiny neon lights, blue and green, yellow and red, orange and purple and . . . Sam turned his eyes from Dolf's and looked instead at his mother scrambling eggs.

'They smell good,' he said.

It wasn't until lunchtime that Sam was able to round up his friends. Dean was late and Hannah was borrowed by the Head of Year to take a visitor to assembly. Only Amy was around, and she whispered to Sam, 'It's all true.'

'I know,' he said.

But by one o'clock they had all gathered in the furthest reaches of the playground, where no one could overhear them, close to the wire fencing that sectioned off the building work. Workmen in high-visibility yellow jackets and hard hats were busily constructing the new extension, laying concrete slabs and carrying bricks around. Machinery whined and buzzed in a wall of sound. For some reason Sam felt safe there. The children settled on a low wall in front of the fencing. They all found they had to shout to be heard.

'The bit I liked best,' Dean said, 'was riding on the dolphin. Yeooooowww! Splash!'

Amy laughed at Dean's noises, which encouraged him to make a few more.

'You can all visit me again tonight,' Amy offered.

'But what I want to know,' Hannah interjected, 'is why. Why can we visit each other's dreams?'

Sam was aware that one of the builders had passed behind them. He turned his head to see a man with a yellow hard hat and grizzled beard hefting a large box.

'Look, everyone,' Sam said. 'I've got a lot to tell you.'

'What?' asked Amy loudly, because at that moment a mobile crane reversed behind them and started making beeping noises.

'Dolf left a hat and glasses in my dream!' Sam shouted.

'I can't hear you!' screamed Hannah.

Sam glanced behind him to see the man with the grizzled beard waving on the crane driver.

'Why don't we go somewhere else?' he mouthed.

'Back to the classroom!' Amy bellowed.

They weren't exactly supposed to be in the classrooms at lunchtime, but neither were they not supposed to be there. It was only a geography classroom and there was nothing valuable in it, just maps on the walls and laminated words saying things like 'river basin' and 'estuary'. When the children arrived, Sam noticed how tidy it was. All the desks were neatly in rows and the chairs were tucked under them. He wondered if there was going to be an inspection like they had had at their old school. Amy was the last in and shut the door behind them. They all sat round a desk at the back, under a word poster saying 'magma'. Sam explained to them about what had happened in his Dream Kingdom, and about the hat and glasses.

'So Dolf visited your Dream Kingdom,' Hannah said slowly. 'And he left something there by accident.'

'The dolls came from Dolf,' Amy added.

'So Dolf *wants* us to visit each other's dreams,' Hannah continued. 'But he doesn't want us to know he's visiting ours.'

'What does "magma" mean?' Dean asked.

Sam ignored him. 'Yeah, I worked all that out. And also I think my mum might be in danger too. Dolf said he'd give her some hypnotherapy.'

'So he can get inside her mind,' Hannah interjected. 'Because maybe the dream dolls only work on children and you have to find other ways of getting to adults.'

'But why?' Sam asked. 'What is Dolf trying to do?'

This was the question that had been plaguing him. He had become certain that Dolf had intentions – evil intentions – towards them. But why?

There was a knock on the classroom door. Then it opened and the builder with the grizzled beard appeared, holding a box full of pipes.

'Is this the geography room?' he asked.

The children nodded.

'Good,' he said. He closed the door behind him, placed the box on the teacher's desk and smiled at Dean. 'Since you asked, magma is a hot liquid below the earth's crust and, when it cools, it forms lava.'

Sam went hot and panicky. The builder had been spying on them, or reading their minds, or something. Dare he look at him to see if he had eyes like Dolf? More and more the half-game they had been playing with each other's dreams was turning real and serious. Summoning all his courage, Sam faced the builder.

No, he was nothing like Dolf. His eyes were blue, kind and wise. And peeping out from his navy overalls was a bright red scarf. He took off his hard hat and displayed a head of iron-grey hair. Feeling bolder, Sam continued to stare at him directly. It was hard to say how old he looked – thirty, fifty, possibly even older. He wore the builders' overalls as though they were a disguise, yet Sam noticed his big brown boots were really muddy at the bottom. The builder had left a trail of mud all over the classroom floor and Sam hoped he wouldn't be blamed for that.

'And your question, Sam, was about Dolf

and his intentions. I only wish I could help you.'

The builder made himself comfortable on the teacher's desk, wriggling out of his high-visibility jacket. Sam glanced at the corridor outside to see if he could spot any real teachers, but no one was about. The children approached the builder slowly. Hannah spoke for all of them.

'Who are you?'

'Sigmund,' the builder replied. 'One of the twelve Guardians of the Gates of Dreams.'

Sam gave a little cough and pinched himself to check he wasn't dreaming right now. He thought he wasn't, but dreams and reality were getting so mixed up he couldn't be sure. There was something about this man Sigmund that commanded his attention. He could tell his friends felt the same. All of them had their eyes trained on him. As he spoke, Sam felt himself become slightly detached, almost as he did in his Dream Kingdom.

'You young people deserve some sort of

explanation,' said Sigmund. 'Allow me. I'll begin at the beginning. Look at that word, "Shingle".' He pointed to another of the word posters. 'Imagine shingle.'

Sam did so. He saw a deserted beach in his mind's eye, and down by the water was the shingle, tiny glistening pebbles that sparkled as the strands of water from the ebbing and flowing tide played among them. He could almost feel the shingle sharp and hard against his bare toes. It was grey and brown and alabaster, and a frond of seaweed waved between two particularly large pebbles.

'Well done,' said Sigmund. 'Is your shingle real?'

'No,' said Sam and Hannah.

'Yes,' said Amy and Dean.

'It's real to you,' Sigmund said, 'and so it's real. It existed for a moment. If you imagine it again, it exists again. So where has it been in the meantime?'

Sam hated it when teachers asked him questions he couldn't answer, and he hoped Sigmund wasn't turning into a teacher.

'The point is,' Sigmund continued, 'that everything you think is real. And so it follows that everything you dream is real. Dreams exist, even more powerfully than thoughts. Your personal dreams are your own reality, where you can be most yourself. You can be whoever you want to be when you dream. All your hopes and fears are there. Yes, your fears.' He paused and eyed Hannah. 'And your future too. That's why, throughout the ages, people have tried to interpret dreams and work out their significance.

'Everyone dreams, even the people who say they don't dream. And not only people, but cats and dogs – all creatures. The whole world dreams. But not all dreams are good. There are some creatures who dream of owning the world and subjecting it to their will. Certain people throughout history have tried. And we believe someone is trying now.'

Sam shuddered. Dolf's face, and particularly his eyes, came into his mind.

'I have eleven brothers and sisters, and together we guard the Gates of Dreams. Because of us, you are safe in your dreams. We make sure your nightmares don't come true, and that your dreams and the real world remain separate. We keep order, but we cannot work alone. That is why we can all enter each other's dreams. We can enter the real world, change our shape and pass undetected.'

Sam checked the trail of mud that Sigmund had left. It had vanished.

'But recently one of our number has barred the gate to his dreams. That fellow Guardian is Dolf Hunter. So I have been following him. I have travelled all over the world in his wake. I arrived here just two days ago. I still do not fully understand why Dolf is here, although I have my suspicions.'

Sam found words were pouring out of him. 'He's a hypnotherapist. He's got a job at my mum's place. He's our lodger. He sleeps in the bedroom next to me. He's going to hypnotise – I mean hypnotherapise – my mum. And he's been invading my dreams!'

'Invading your dreams?'

Rapidly the children brought Sigmund up to date. Sam realised that they shared his instinctive trust of Sigmund. He knew here was the man who could help them.

'*I* think,' Hannah said, 'that Dolf wants to control us in some way. Because he gave Amy the doll, didn't he? So he must have wanted to get into *her* dreams. And when he sent Sam upstairs for those photos, he *knew* Sam would see the dolls and be tempted to take some. And he's been in Sam's dream and left the hat and glasses there.'

'You're a sharp young lady,' Sigmund said. Hannah blushed with pleasure. 'But what I want to find out is why Dolf should be interested in you four children, if you'll excuse me. Unless there's something he wants or needs. Or unless there's something special about you. I wonder . . .'

His voice trailed away. Everyone was silent.

'What we need to do,' Sigmund continued, 'is find some way of getting into Dolf's Dream Kingdom to see what he's up to.'

'But you said he'd barred the gate!' Amy reminded him.

'True, true. All too true.'

'I know!' said Dean. 'Sam must put one of the dolls under *Dolf's* pillow!'

'A bright idea,' Sigmund said. 'I can see you're one to watch. But unfortunately the dolls are in thrall to Dolf, and they would let him know what you are trying to do.'

Everyone was stumped. Sam remarked sadly, 'Without the dolls, we can't do it.'

Then Hannah said, 'I didn't put a doll under

my pillow last night.'

The significance hit Sam immediately. 'But you were still in our dreams. So how? What—'

'That's possible,' Sigmund explained. 'There are channels between Dream Kingdoms. A small coincidence of time or place or mood can bring two Dream Kingdoms close together. I'm not surprised that Hannah could travel into her friends' dreams. Clearly the ties between you are very close, possibly closer than you might realise. Interesting. And you say Dolf's been visiting your dreams.' Sigmund stroked his grizzled chin.

'He's certainly been in my Dream Kingdom,' said Sam.

'And when everyone left me last night,' Amy said, 'my sweet and sour sauce turned all sour. That might have been Dolf. But then it turned sweet again.'

'Evidence, indeed,' Sigmund said. 'And Dean? Hannah? Has he been in your kingdoms?'

'I don't think so,' Dean said.

Hannah was silent. Sigmund looked at her.

'I don't remember,' she said. 'I remember nothing.'

Those words sounded familiar to Sam but he couldn't think why.

'We have a puzzle here,' Sigmund said. 'Dolf won't let his brothers and sisters into his dreams, but he is entering the dreams of you young people. You are clearly part of his plans. He might actually want you to visit his Dream Kingdom. In that case, you must not. No, you must not.'

'But, Sigmund,' Sam found himself saying, 'is there anyone who's able to go and spy on Dolf?'

Sigmund shook his head and looked stern. 'No,' he said. 'No one.'

'But we might be able to,' Sam persisted.

'You might.'

'Then we could start by getting the key that lets us into Dolf's kingdom. That might be useful.'

Sigmund eyed Sam narrowly. 'You are a brave young man. But I forbid—'

At that moment the classroom door opened and Sam's teacher appeared.

'What *are* you doing in here?' she demanded in her permanently harassed voice.

Sam looked to Sigmund to offer an explanation. After all, he was the adult. Adults always listened to other adults, or pretended to.

'Come on! Out!' the teacher shouted.

That's odd, thought Sam. She's looking at Sigmund as if she's seeing straight through him. The children got up from their seats and filed out of the classroom. Sam cast a glance behind him. The room was empty, except for a shadow that momentarily darkened the wall. There, on the desk, was the box of pipes.

Out in the corridor the children were silent for a moment. Then the bell clanged for the end of lunch.

'See you at midnight!' Sam said to Dean.

'You bet,' Dean said.

'And you too, Hannah.'

She said nothing. But when Sam looked at her, he could swear there were tears in her eyes. Why? What did Hannah know that they didn't?

Chapter Six

The greenbirds were making a racket. They were chattering, their wooden beaks were clattering, and it struck Sam that they sounded very much like an approaching mechanical train. But if it was an approaching mechanical train, there would be a problem, because there was no station in Sam's Dream Kingdom, no track and no ticket office.

Correction: there was a ticket office. One had appeared just by the Shooting Stone. It was a green wooden hut with a counter, behind which was a gentleman in a white bowler hat. Sam handed over what money he had in his pocket and the man gave Sam a string of red liquorice. This was all very enjoyable, Sam thought, but he was dimly aware of having to go somewhere and do something, although he couldn't remember what it was.

The train arrived and he boarded it. It was a

small wooden train, the sort you get in large parks to take you from one end to the other. Sam settled on a seat by the window and looked out at his Dream Kingdom, which began to move faster and faster in front of his eyes until it became a blur of trees and river and more trees. The next thing he heard was Dean's voice.

'Hold on tight!' he shouted.

Sam discovered that he was now on a roller-coaster which was plunging down, then slowly ascending, and then was poised, dangling perilously, at the top. Below was what looked like a bottomless pit. Even though he knew that he was dreaming, Sam was breathless, with a feeling somewhere in between fear and excitement. Then everything went dark.

No, not dark. In fact there was blazing sunshine, the sort you have to screw your eyes in if you want to see anything. Sam was going round and round and round on a big wheel. Earth changed to sky and sky changed to earth in quick succession. After a while the wheel came to a stop at the very top and Sam discovered that he was not alone. With him, in the boat of the big wheel, suspended over a noisy, colourful fairground, were Dean, Amy and Hannah. Sam was relieved to see them but a bit confused by all the changes in the past few moments. Even for a dream, a lot had been going on.

'This is my Dream Kingdom,' Dean said.

Sam tried to survey it, but it was difficult to see much. As soon as you looked down and tried to focus on one thing, the dodgems, or the roller-coaster, or the ghost train, it swam in front of your eyes and vanished, to be replaced by something else. Sam thought he saw a hippopotamus and a Land-Rover. Then the big wheel started turning again, slowly, then faster and faster, and Sam thought he heard Hannah scream.

Next thing he knew, they were in the ghost

train. He felt sick and giddy. They all hurtled through the blackness and Sam saw two metal doors in front of them. They opened in the nick of time. Their carriage rushed on, then came to a stop over a pit of boiling red liquid.

'Magma,' said Dean.

Another quick change, and Sam and his friends were in a dodgem car and Dean was driving, taking them at a breathless speed towards other cars, then straight towards the sides, until Amy shouted that she wanted a rest.

'I know where we can rest,' Dean said.

He pushed the car harder and harder and Sam could see in front of them something that looked like a little oasis, with a lake and palm trees and four striped deckchairs. It looked enticing. Sam could feel them all willing and wishing to be there. The car went faster and faster. But the faster it went, the further away the oasis seemed to be. And then they were in a vast, noisy canteen, like the school canteen only bigger and booming. A red-faced dinner lady asked Sam what he wanted to eat.

'Chips,' he said.

'Sorry,' came her voice, which was not her voice but a voice that was all too familiar. 'We only have eggs.' It was Dolf's voice.

Dolf was here, or had been here. Had he got there before them and closed up the channel? Sam looked round urgently but it was impossible to make out anyone in the press of bodies. He wished desperately he could be somewhere quieter and less busy. And then he was in the lobby of a huge office block, on a black leather settee, with his friends by his side. Amy looked as startled as he felt, but Dean seemed to be asleep now. He was slumped by the side of the settee, his eyes closed, his mouth slightly agape. Hannah was white-faced and silent. Sam found his mind was clearing and he remembered what they were all supposed to be doing. They were to find a way to Dolf's Dream Kingdom.

'But we'll never find anything in Dean's Dream Kingdom,' he said. 'And even if we did, we'd never stay still long enough to have a look at it.'

'I don't think you could get into Dolf's Dream Kingdom through Dean's,' Amy continued. 'Dean is so exciting and Dolf is dull.'

These were odd words but it was a dream and Sam knew exactly what she meant, only Dean's Dream Kingdom was exciting in a wrong sort of way. No wonder he was exhausted now. 'So if it's no use looking in Dean's kingdom, and there isn't a channel in mine or yours, Amy, then we must look in Hannah's.

'No,' Hannah said.

'But we must,' Amy said kindly. 'It's the only way to get to Dolf secretly.'

'No,' said Hannah.

Sam thought maybe she was embarrassed about her Dream Kingdom. Hannah could be a bossy girl at times, and maybe there were parts of her she didn't want her friends to see. Her Dream Kingdom might be like a school, or the army, and Hannah would be in charge. But they had to go there anyway.

'We don't mind what your kingdom is like, Hannah.'

'No,' she said.

'No!' said the receptionist behind the gleaming metallic desk. 'No!' struck the large clock in the lobby. 'No!' whistled the wind which blew through the revolving doors.

'Why?' demanded Sam.

'Because I only ever have nightmares,' said Hannah, trembling.

Her words sent a chill through Sam. It was as if he could feel her fear like cobweb fingers stroking his arm. He wasn't even sure whether he wanted to go to Hannah's kingdom now. In his hesitation, he glanced around him at the lobby they were seated in. To their left were three lifts, and every so often crowds of people were disgorged and then more got in. To his right were the smoked-glass doors of the entrance. Above them was a large window. Sam noticed that it had got dark while they were sitting there. The sky was lowering and black clouds, darker than the navy sky, seemed to press down on his vision. It was a horrible, menacing sky, and thoughts entered Sam's mind like, *It's the end of the world* and *They're coming to get you*. Words like *disease* and *vermin* and *earthquake* danced in front of his eyes. Very scared now, he looked up for help to the receptionist behind the desk. The receptionist? There was no receptionist, but a wild, mad woman with greasy, lank grey hair and a mouth that gaped and dribbled. She leered wickedly at the children, then laughed. Sam didn't exactly think she was going to eat them, but she wanted to get them.

She called out in a hoarse, evil voice,

'Welcome to Hannah's Nightmare Kingdom!'

'Quick!' Sam shouted. 'Wake Dean and let's get out of here!'

Amy shook Dean, who opened his eyes blearily. He came to consciousness in time to join the others, who, with one will, were running over to the lifts. They seemed safer somehow than the dark outdoors. A lift opened in front of them. To Sam's surprise it was empty. They piled in, the doors closed and off they went.

The lift shook and banged its way up the shaft far too quickly for Sam's liking. He'd never been particularly scared of lifts before but this one was different. He was sure a cable was loose – it would snap and they would all hurtle down and smash into the basement. Or maybe they would go too fast and crash into the roof. He wished it would stop, but it just went on and on, for much longer than a lift ought to. On and on. Would they ever get out? Or was the lift out of control? He realised then that it was, and even though it was in Hannah's dream, she couldn't control it either. That was the truly terrifying thing. They were all powerless.

The lift finally shuddered and slowed. Sam reckoned they must be on the top floor. It felt like they'd travelled up forty or fifty storeys. The lift doors opened, but they were still trapped. An old, wooden door was in front of them, tightly jammed. Sam tugged on the handle. It wasn't going to open.

'The lift's moving again!' Amy shouted.

'I don't like this,' Dean said.

The lift shot to the right and out on to the roof. Yes, they were very high up, miles up, and the lift had become glass. Around them were all the surrounding city roofs, a collection of black, metallic, spiky skyscrapers. Sam knew they were not safe. Not at all safe. And the lift careered onwards, as if it had a mind of its own. It shot into the air and

Sam made the mistake of looking down. His stomach lurched as he saw the distance between him and the ground, where tiny cars and buses looked like gnats or fleas.

A moment later they were inside again, but all Sam's sense of direction had left him. The lift capsule had now changed into a train and was chugging slowly along a wide tunnel. The walls were made of dirty white tiles. Sam saw the occasional rat scuttle across the tracks.

'Where are we going?' he asked Hannah.

'Home,' she said.

That was encouraging. They reached a platform and finally got out of the lift. They ran down a flight of stairs and found they were outside a large, dilapidated block of flats. They looked familiar to Sam. He was certain they were near his home, but he couldn't be sure. He looked around him. It was and it wasn't his town. Or rather, the houses *felt* like the houses in Hannah's road but *looked* different. Then he thought he heard someone running behind them.

'He's coming!' Hannah muttered.

Sam looked over his shoulder. In the distance was the figure of a man who was gaining on them. Icy fear trickled down Sam's brow. Terror welled like sick in his stomach. He had to get away – they all had to get away.

'Run!' he screamed.

But his voice was strangled by his throat and only a squeak emerged. He started running anyway and knew the others were running too. Not fast enough, though. The man was closer. Sam was too scared to look to check. There was Hannah's house in front of them. A demonic laugh was at his shoulder now.

'Help!' he tried to shout.

He was so frightened now that he wanted someone, anyone, to come to his aid. But again his throat didn't work. No sound would come out. He redoubled his effort. He heard himself whimper.

It was all right. Hannah had got them in. They were all in her house now, safe. But no, not safe. The man was at the window now, banging on it repeatedly. Bang, bang, like a hammer on an anvil. It was only a matter of time before he smashed the window and got them. They were not safe and would never be safe. Bang. Louder now. BANG. Sam was paralysed with fear. He stared at the man. He was big and burly and wore a red-check shirt. His cheeks were red with the effort of striking on the window. And his eyes were fierce and determined. Flat and yellow. Because they weren't his eyes. They were Dolf's eyes. Because the man was Dolf. Sam knew that now, and was certain that Hannah's nightmare had revealed Dolf in his true colours – as a destroyer.

BANG. BANG. An enormous crash. The window exploded into a million shards of glass. Sam threw himself down onto the settee and buried his face in the red throw. He realised that with his right hand he was grasping something: a cool, hard, round thing. It made the darkness inside his head a little clearer. And he saw something: a grey landscape, with hills rising and falling, and a large, dome-shaped temple in the distance.

He heard a piercing scream. It was from Amy. Something terrible must be happening to her. Dolf had got her. Her screaming became louder and louder and he could feel her shaking. But no, it was his alarm clock that was shaking and ringing furiously. The dream was over.

First Sam felt nothing but relief. In a trice this was replaced by a sharp anxiety. In his dream, he had found something very important. The point was, did he still have it?

Yes. The cold, egg-shaped thing was still in his hand. He knew instinctively what it was. He had the key to Dolf's Dream Kingdom.

Chapter Seven

Lying in bed, Sam tried to remember in as much detail as possible what had happened in the dream. He was surprised how vividly everything was coming back to him. The madness of Dean's fairground rides seemed as nothing compared to the terror of Hannah's kingdom. Sam wondered if she dreamed like that every night, and why. Finally he recalled grasping the egg-shaped thing, which was now held tightly in his hand. He brought it out of the bedclothes to look at it closely.

He recognised it immediately and was filled with disappointment. Fully awake now, he knew that it wasn't the key to Dolf's Dream Kingdom after all. It was a present that his mother had given Hannah's mother some months ago. In fact Sam had chosen it in the gift shop they had been in. Hannah's mother collected little marble eggs of all sizes and kept them in a porcelain bowl on the mantelpiece. Sam had often noticed them. This particular egg was stone-grey, flecked with black. Even though he had been holding it tightly, it was still cool to his touch, as marble was. It had clearly fallen down the side of Hannah's settee and he had found it last night.

But wait. He wasn't in Hannah's living room last night. He had been here, in his own bed. Yet this was Hannah's mother's egg, he was sure of it. He felt his heart racing. Then he stiffened as he heard sounds from next door. Dolf was moving about, getting ready to come down for breakfast. Sam resolved to eat his own breakfast as quickly as possible and leg it to school, where he could find his friends and, most importantly, Sigmund.

In the kitchen his mother was sitting drinking coffee at the table. She was dressed in a plain black dress, with only a hint of make-up.

'What's wrong?' he asked her.

'Nothing,' she replied. She gave him a faint smile.

'Why are you dressed like that?'

'Like what?' The way she looked vaguely at herself reminded him of his old, scatty mum. 'Oh, this dress. I don't know. I found it at the back of my wardrobe and thought I'd wear it today.'

'It doesn't suit you,' Sam said.

'I think it does,' his mum replied. 'It makes me look more . . . more reasonable. And suitable.'

'Has Phoebe come back?' Sam asked.

The cat had been gone for more than a day. She was always a wanderer, but she had never stayed away this long before.

'No,' his mum replied. 'But it's . . . it's tidier without her.'

At that moment Dolf entered. Sam noticed the way his mother's eyes travelled immediately to Dolf's, almost as if she was waiting for instructions.

'Good morning,' she said.

'Good morning,' he replied.

'I'll make your breakfast,' she said. 'Eggs.'

'Eggs,' he echoed, and Sam was aware that Dolf was probing him.

There was a pressure in his head, and it felt as though something was pushing among his brain cells, hunting for something. He was looking for knowledge of the egg. Sam knew what to do – he had to have a thought so vivid that it would dazzle and blind Dolf. So, swift as light, he imagined himself back in Dean's fairground. He was zooming down on the roller-coaster, swinging high on the big wheel, chasing other cars on the dodgems.

Dolf winced and put his hand to his forehead. Sam's plan had worked.

'I'm not hungry,' Sam said to his mother. 'Gotta go.'

Grabbing his school bag, he was out of the house and haring along the road in an instant.

*

He was early for school. He waited by the entrance to the Year 7 block, looking out anxiously for his friends. It had begun to rain, not heavily but persistently. He found himself yawning. He guessed the dreams last night meant he hadn't had much real rest. But the funny thing was, everyone he saw coming into school seemed rather tired that morning. Or simply quiet. Even Katie and Lauren and Emma and Claire just threw him a careless glance, all four together, in unison. Three teachers walked in beside them, each in step with the other. They were holding black A4 folders thick with papers. He spotted Amy behind them. She came straight up to him.

'Are you all right?' she asked. 'How's Hannah?'

'I haven't seen her yet. I escaped. I found something,' Sam told her. 'A marble egg. I think it's some sort of key.'

'I saw something,' she said. 'There was a picture in Hannah's room. It was of a grey land with a big temple with a round roof.'

Sam was so interested in what she was saying he didn't notice Mr Pearson, the Head, approach them.

'Amy!' he said. 'You were talking to Sam just then. What were you talking about?'

Amy never spoke to any of the teachers, ever. And hardly any of the other pupils. Sam understood why the Head was interested that she was speaking to him.

Amy was silent.

'Sam, can you tell me what she was saying?'

How could he? He shook his head. But he wasn't too worried. Mr Pearson was a kind man. He huffed and puffed a bit at the school villains, and threatened the school occasionally when there was an epidemic of bad behaviour, but most of the time he had a smile for you, and he knew nearly everybody's name. Even the Year 7s.

'I need to know what Amy Wong was saying to you, Sam,' the head repeated.

'It was nothing, sir,' Sam said.

'I need to know what Amy Wong was saying to you.' Then the Head looked slightly puzzled. 'Did I just repeat myself? How odd! My apologies – I must be overtired. I was up late last night – governors' meeting. Never mind.' The Head rushed off. For a minute Sam thought he had imagined that strange encounter.

As they entered their classroom, Sam and Amy swapped notes about their dreams and found their memories were identical. They looked around for Dean, but he had not arrived. Nor had Hannah. After last night, Sam was worried.

Sam couldn't concentrate all morning. In between waiting for Hannah and Dean, and hoping to spot Sigmund, he was completely distracted. His mind wandered back to his dreams of the night before and then forward to what he would say to Sigmund. As yet, the building work outside hadn't started. Perhaps the rain meant that the contractors wouldn't be coming today. This alarmed Sam. He didn't fancy sleeping that night without having had some guidance from Sigmund. He knew that things were getting serious.

By lunchtime neither of his friends had arrived. He was waiting to consult with Amy, who was late back from swimming. Then, to his relief, he saw Dean approaching. His hair was plastered to his head. The rain was heavy now.

'Where have you been?' Sam asked him.

'To the doctor,' he said. 'My mum took me. I have to take some medicine.'

'Medicine? What for? You're not ill.'

'I know, but it's because I don't concentrate at school. They said it'll stop me being naughty and make me settle down.'

'You mean they're going to drug you?'

'I didn't like Hannah's Dream Kingdom,' Dean said. 'That lift—' He broke off to give a fair imitation of how it shot out of the building and onto the roof. He made a weird, screeching sound.

'Dean Matthews!' shouted one of the French teachers who was passing by. 'Stop making that dreadful noise. At once. We will have no more disorderly conduct!' And she sailed off.

'Have you seen Hannah?' Sam asked Dean.

'No,' he said. 'Maybe she's gone to Dolf's kingdom. And been eaten alive. I'm hungry. I want to go and get some chips.' He raced off.

Sam was troubled now. Hannah's non-appearance at school was a first. Since her parents were teachers and she was good at schoolwork, she never missed a day, even when Katie and Lauren and Emma and Claire were getting at her. He consulted his watch. If he ran all the way to Hannah's, he might be able to get there and back before afternoon lessons. If he was late – well, he'd decide what to do about that if it happened. He needed to see Hannah anyway, as there was no sign of the builders, or of Sigmund. He hunched his shoulders, lowered his head to avoid the driving rain and ran.

He rang a couple of times at Hannah's doorbell and was just about to turn away in frustration when he heard some noises from inside. The door opened, but only a little way as someone had attached a chain to it.

'Who's there?' came Hannah's voice.

'Me,' Sam said.

Hannah disengaged the chain and let Sam in. It was very, very strange, being in her front room. It was almost like being back in their dream. Now it felt as though Hannah's room looked wrong and their dream was the right version. Sam shivered involuntarily. Then he looked at Hannah. She was pale and unhappy.

'Why weren't you at school?' he asked.

'When I woke up, I was screaming and crying. My mum took my temperature and she said I had a fever. So I have to stay off school until it comes down. If it doesn't, she's going to take me to the doctor.'

'Dean's been to the doctor,' Sam said. 'They're going to give him drugs.'

'It's OK. I'm not really ill. Come and sit down.'

She went over to the settee and Sam hesitated. He remembered the nightmare and how they had all buried themselves in the settee when Dolf was banging on the window. But Hannah didn't seem scared now, so he couldn't show he was nervous. He sat down next to her, feeling the springs of the settee cutting into him. He brought the marble egg out of his pocket.

'Is this your mum's?' he asked Hannah.

Hannah took it from him and examined it. 'I think it might be one of hers, but I'm not sure. It feels very cold. Maybe I still have a temperature.' Then Hannah frowned, as if she was remembering something.

'It shouldn't be cold,' Sam said. 'I've had it in my pocket all day.' He explained to Hannah how he had found it in their dream when he was lying on the settee. He told her how he and Amy saw a grey land and a temple. 'I think this might be the key, even if it doesn't look like one. But we need to find Sigmund and tell him.'

'Sam,' Hannah said suddenly, 'do you think we're letting our imaginations run away with us?'

'What do you mean?'

'That none of this is true.'

'No, it has to be true. We all dreamed the same thing. Sigmund was real.'

'I know it feels that way, but maybe it was *us* who made it happen. Like when everyone around you believes something, you can't help going along with them and believing it yourself. You know, like sometimes when you're at a football match and everyone is shouting and you find you're shouting too, even though you didn't mean to? Like that. Or maybe we're all making ourselves think the Dream Kingdoms are real because we want to, as we have boring lives. Or something . . .'

'Hannah,' Sam asked her, 'are you scared?'

She didn't reply, but she didn't need to. Sam found that since they had all started sharing dreams, he and his friends had become closer. He was able to sense their feelings even more than before. He knew that Hannah didn't want the Dream Kingdoms to be true because she couldn't cope unless things were concrete and real and she could control them. He also knew she was embarrassed at her own Dream Kingdom, and that her friends had seen her worst fears. She liked them to admire her; she feared they didn't now. Sam knew all this and he wanted to reassure her.

'I think you're the bravest of all of us,' he

said. 'To let someone into your nightmares takes real guts. Anyway, you can't help your fears. No one can.'

'But you're not afraid,' Hannah said to him.

'That's not true!' Sam replied. 'Ever since this whole thing began, I've never been more scared in my life. And listen, Hannah, my mum's changing. Since Dolf's been living with us, she's got duller and duller. I don't know why. And even school seems different. I'm beginning to think that something is happening that is much more important than the four of us, and I am frightened. But I suppose what I think is, we have no choice. We have to carry on with this adventure. No – there is a choice. We can do it and be terrified, or do it pretending to be brave. I'm going to try to pretend to be brave.'

Hannah nodded. 'Sometimes,' she said, 'if you pretend to be something, you are really that thing. When I was the queen in the school play at

Park Place Primary, when I was on the stage I felt like a queen.'

'Yes, that's right. We have to act.'

Sam and Hannah grinned at each other. Sam realised also that he couldn't do this without his friends. Their trust in him made him want to be brave.

'We have to find Sigmund,' Sam said.

'He'll find us. He'll know we have the key – if it is the key, and not just one of my mum's eggs. The thing is, I remember nothing.' Hannah frowned again, looking as if she were in pain. Gradually her brow cleared. 'No, I remember something. I had a dream. I was in our room, here, and a man came, and dropped an egg – this egg – in my mum's bowl. And I was scared. Sam, Dolf planted it here!'

'All the more reason to find Sigmund,' Sam replied. 'I'd better get back to school as soon as possible.'

'Would you like something to eat first? I was going to make some sandwiches.' She attempted a smile. 'Not egg.'

Sam grinned back at her, then said, 'Hannah, I've got a question. Do you always have nightmares?'

Hannah stopped on the way to the kitchen and began to play with a piece of her hair. 'I think so, as far back as I can remember. I used to be scared of going to sleep and so I'd just read books late into the night.'

'Did that bullying last year make your nightmares worse?'

'No,' Hannah replied. 'The funny thing was, it made it better. When I'm most unhappy, my dreams are better. It's only when things are OK that the bad dreams start. I don't understand that.'

Sam didn't either and reflected how little he did understand about what was going on. All the more reason to stick to one thing at a time. And his first task was to find Sigmund.

He got back to school in the nick of time and saw immediately that the builders must be having a day off. His first afternoon lesson was science. He and Amy went to the chemistry labs together, and he filled her in on the important details of his visit to Hannah's. When they arrived at the labs, they saw their normal teacher wasn't there. Instead they had a supply teacher. Sam was fed up. Whenever there was a supply teacher, some of the kids in his class messed around, seeing how far they could go. Then the supply teacher would get annoyed and start handing out punishments right, left and centre. The other week Sam had been given a detention by a supply even though he was only whispering to the boy next to him. This supply teacher was reading the lesson notes left by the regular teacher and not paying too much attention to the pupils filing in. It didn't look promising.

'Open your text book to the chapter on cells,' the supply teacher said. 'Page 53. You'll see some diagrams. Copy them into your exercise books and label them correctly. Oh, and . . .'

He paused. That made everyone look up. He was a dark-haired, middle-aged man who wore a pair of heavily framed spectacles. His jacket was corduroy and his shirt maroon. His scarlet tie clashed with it. He peered at the class through his spectacles and then removed them to have a good look round at everyone. Oh dear, thought Sam, he won't survive a minute here. He could already hear his classmates giggling. But as the supply teacher surveyed them, the giggling subsided. One by one they settled down to work. Sam was mystified and glanced at Amy, who shrugged.

Sam began to copy the diagrams and saw the teacher leave the bench and begin to walk about, observing the class working. He came over to Sam.

'Good,' he said. 'That's the ticket.'

There was a click as the hand of the clock on the wall slotted into the hour. Two o'clock. Sam was overcome with a wave of tiredness and then suddenly was wide awake. But the rest of the class had frozen in time. Like statues, they had stopped in the middle of whatever they were doing, pens in mid-air, turning over a page, scratching their heads. Only Amy was moving, leaving her stool and coming towards him.

'That's the ticket,' said the supply teacher again. 'The ticket, or the key – it doesn't matter which. You see, if you possess an item from someone else's Dream Kingdom, you may enter it. The egg you found, Sam, belongs in Dolf's Dream Kingdom. You've succeeded in finding the key, or Dolf has succeeded in giving it to you.'

'Sigmund!' Sam exclaimed.

'Yes, it's me.'

'Is Dolf's Dream Kingdom the one with grey hills and a temple?' Amy asked.

'Are the hills grey now? I recall a time when they were fresh and green. How sad. How very sad.'

'We must be able to do something to turn them back again,' Sam said.

'Too dangerous,' Sigmund said.

For a minute Sam thought Sigmund sounded like his mother. Adults were always saying things were too dangerous, but sometimes they turned out not to be. Sam found himself saying, 'If I've got the key, I can go there. And I will.'

'No,' Sigmund said.

'It's our only chance,' Sam said. 'Tell me how I use the key. Tell me.'

'Dream tonight and keep the egg with you. Once you arrive in your own Dream Kingdom, look for a well. Draw up the bucket and place the egg in it. Lower the bucket and see what happens.'

It was strange, but Sam felt as if he had forced Sigmund to give him this information, as though he had some sort of power. He started to tremble. He didn't fully understand what was going on.

'Do I do the same?' asked Amy. 'Is there a well in my kingdom?'

'No, Amy,' Sigmund replied. 'If more than one person invades Dolf's Dream Kingdom, your thought communications will alert him to your presence. Sam might be able to slip in undetected. I say *might*. Besides, we cannot afford to lose you too. Sam, the risks are great.'

'I know,' said Sam. 'But it will be all right.' He said that partly to reassure Sigmund and partly to reassure himself.

Sigmund looked surprised, then was silent, deep in thought, as he examined Sam.

'Then you must go. But be alert to your own safety. And Amy, it is imperative you stay in your own Dream Kingdom. If you sense Sam is in danger, you may be able to assist him.'

'How?' asked Amy.

'Dream and send your dream to him. If he is in grave danger, bring him into your dream.' Sigmund now addressed Sam. 'And you, young man, must take careful note of everything you see. Give me your hand.'

Sam held out his hand to Sigmund. The Dream Guardian pressed his forefinger into Sam's palm. As he did so, a golden sheen materialised. Fully developed, it almost blinded Sam and Amy. Quickly it faded to nothing.

'This will give you a degree of protection. And also it will enable you to transmit your observations safely back to me,' Sigmund said. 'I need to see the same things as you do, so I can begin to work out what Dolf has in mind. Unfortunately I cannot send messages to you, as they would be picked up. I wouldn't let you do this, Sam, unless I believed the greater danger is that you don't go on this mission. I fear the world is no longer safe.'

'What will happen to Sam if the mission goes wrong?' Amy asked, and Sam wished she hadn't.

'His mind will never be his own again.'

'Like a zombie,' Amy said.

'A zombie?' Sam began, and then the three of them started as the door opened. In a split second Sam saw the Head of Year standing there, heard the hands of the clock disengage, sensed movement around him, and it was all as if the last few moments had never happened.

'That's the ticket,' the supply teacher said. 'When you've finished see if you can answer the questions about the differences between animal cells and plant cells.'

'Are they behaving?' asked the Head of Year.

'Perfectly,' said Sigmund.

Chapter Eight

Sam lay on his side in bed, his knees pulled up to his chest, preparing himself for going to sleep. It felt more as if he was going on a journey. First he checked the egg was safe, but he already knew it was. He had had the foresight to realise that he could not go to sleep holding the egg, as it would slip from his fingers as his hand relaxed, so he had devised an ingenious contraption. He had filched the little green bag containing the Scrabble letters from the toy box downstairs and put the egg in that. He had then threaded a ribbon from his mum's sewing kit through it and tied the ribbon round his neck. He slipped the bag with the egg under the neck of his pyjamas, certain that this way it would travel with him.

Now that all he had to do was go to sleep he felt very, very lonely. So far on his dream adventures he had known his friends would be there. Although it was true that Amy was with him in spirit, he had not told either Hannah or Dean what he was about to do – Hannah, because she needed to get her strength back and Dean because . . . Sam had to admit that on a mission of this delicacy, Dean was not the right person to have around. Sigmund had emphasised that Sam's role was simply to spy and spies have to be secretive.

Enough thinking about his mission, Sam told himself. In order to fall asleep, he had to focus on something else. He decided to think about his mother. She was fretting when she came back from work as Rahila the acupuncturist had lost a picture of her father in India and was very upset. Sam's mum had been helping her find it and was late home. Then she spent hours looking at a catalogue because the staff at Avalon were going to wear uniforms, so they would look more respectable, Sam's mum said. White aprons maybe, or white house coats, snow white. And the seven dwarfs, Sam said to himself, realising that the logic of his thoughts was breaking up and that he was on his way to his Dream Kingdom.

He was lying on his side on a log. When he opened his eyes a bright white light dazzled him. It was coming from a tall lamp that was trained on his eyes. It was something that shouldn't be in his kingdom, so Sam frowned at it and it shrivelled into a twig. A greenbird flew down from a nearby tree, picked it up in its beak and flew away with it. Another greenbird came and used its wooden beak to send a Morse code message.

'How old are you, Sam?' it asked.

'One hundred and twenty-three,' Sam replied.

Then he was aware of something bumping against his chest and felt to see what it was. The egg. The pleasant inconsequentiality of his dream fell away and Sam remembered all too clearly what he had to do. His memory drained his Dream Kingdom of colour. The multicoloured leaves were blackened now. The greenbirds turned a dull olive. There was no movement in his forest, as if the trees and undergrowth were bracing themselves for a storm.

Just as he expected, he saw a well. The stone was mossy and weathered. Sam wondered why he had never noticed it before. He walked over to it, crunching leaves which sang discordant notes. He pulled on the damp, thick rope and soon saw a bucket come into view. He removed the egg from its pouch and placed it carefully at the base of the bucket. There was a small clunking sound. Then he lowered it, feeling oddly bereft without the egg. He had not let it out of his sight since finding it on Hannah's settee. It was beginning to be part of him.

The bucket slid lower and lower and then

could no longer be seen. Then Sam heard a faint splash as it made contact with the water. A splash, and then a churning sound, followed by what sounded like a rush of water. There was a gurgle and slapping against the side of the well. Now Sam could see that the water level was rising rapidly. Was it going to overflow and drown his Dream Kingdom?

No. It stopped when it reached the top. The egg had floated free of the bucket and was bobbing on the surface. That's strange, Sam thought. Marble shouldn't float. It's far too heavy. Maybe the egg was made of chalk or polystyrene. He needed to check. So he leaned over the edge of the well to try to grasp the egg. But he leaned too far, overbalanced and toppled head first into the water.

It was surprisingly warm, as warm as a bath. Sam felt himself dragged lower and lower, as if he was being sucked down. To his relief, he saw the egg and reached out for it. He grabbed it and held it tight. As he did so he felt himself corkscrew round and round, round and round, becoming dizzier and dizzier, dizzier and dizzier. When he came to, he was at the bottom of the shaft of the well on some dry, dusty ground.

He sat up and looked around him. He seemed to be in an underground cavern. The walls were of rock and some rough stones littered the ground. He couldn't work out where the light was coming from which enabled him to see. That scared him, but he remembered that he was determined to act as if he was brave, even if he wasn't really. Now he was here – wherever 'here' was – he would have to get on with his spying mission. He tightened his hand to check the egg was still there.

It had gone.

Frantic, Sam searched everywhere. Then it dawned on him that maybe the egg had served its purpose. It had vanished because he was now in

Dolf's Dream Kingdom. This empty cavern was it, or at least part of it. With caution, Sam began to explore his surroundings. The walls were solid rock and so was the roof. It was impossible to see how he could have arrived. Then he noticed an iron gate at one end, apparently leading to blackness. He made his way there and pushed at the gate. With a sigh, it eased itself open. Summoning all his resolve, Sam felt his way into the tunnel.

It was completely black in there, a thick, woolly blackness that he could almost touch. He edged his way along, feeling the sides of the walls with his hands. The stone felt a bit like the hard marble of the egg. Soon he noticed that the darkness was getting thinner. Some way in front of and above him was a dim light. Encouraged, he pressed on towards it. Eventually he was standing under the source of the light. There was an opening above him, but his way was blocked by a thick mesh of wire.

Sam tried to push it up. It wouldn't budge. He tried making a hole between the wires with his bare hands, but that proved impossible too. Remembering that he was in his own dream, Sam tried imagining the mesh shifting, but that didn't work either. Then he thought he detected a sound, a kind of thump, thump, thump, getting closer and closer. The ground above him began to shake. The thumping was louder now. Suddenly the light was blotted out as a black shape appeared on the mesh and then vanished. Another appeared and vanished. They were the soles of boots, Sam realised, tramping along the ground. A troop of men was marching above him. Quaking, Sam pinned himself to the side of the tunnel.

Once they had gone, he examined the wire mesh. It was definitely looser now. With a huge effort he prised some wires apart and found that he was able to wriggle enough to get his head through the hole and see around him.

It was definitely Dolf's Dream Kingdom – at least, it was the kingdom he had seen the previous night. There were the grey hills and the grey, lowering sky, and in the distance he could see a column of soldiers marching away from him along a straight, wide road. He heard a rumbling to his left and saw a railway track, where grey, egg-shaped carriages made of marble were trundling in the same direction as the soldiers. Every so often they stopped.

Stretching even more, Sam found he was able to get his shoulders and arms out of the tunnel and then it was an easy matter to get the rest of his body out. Standing upright now, he quickly surveyed the land and could see no living creature. There were just flat, grey hills which merged imperceptibly with the dense, grey sky. The land was entirely featureless. The air was chill and damp. Sam felt oppressed in some way and also exposed, aware that if he were spotted he would be in mortal danger. He had to hide. He ran over to the railway track, where he thought there might be cover from the passing carriages. He noticed that they were open on one side and it was a simple matter to jump inside when they came to a halt. The carriage he found himself in was completely empty. It was about two metres long and nearly a metre high, enough for a fully grown person to lie down in. Sam crouched at the bottom of the cold marble.

Within a few moments, it seemed, the light diminished and Sam reckoned the carriage had entered some kind of enclosed space. Then it came to a stop. He lifted himself up and peered around. There was a platform, so he got out and scurried quickly towards some metal steps going up the side of a wall. Finding that his legs had a mind of their own, he ran higher and higher without looking until he reached a balcony sectioned off by an iron balustrade.

He was poised above a vast hall. Below were

rows and rows of people, some sitting and eating, some at computer stations and some taking part in a series of exercises, squatting and raising themselves. There were people sleeping in dormitories, people standing under showers washing and people marching and banging rhythmically on drums. What struck Sam was not the sheer numbers – there must have been about ten thousand people down there – but that everyone was doing the same things. Blocks of people acting in unison, all bending at the same time, all raising a spoon to their lips at the same time, all turning in their sleep at the same time. For a moment Sam thought they must be robots, but something told him that they weren't.

Directly opposite him, on the other side of the vast hall, Sam saw a row of large smoked-glass windows. He thought he could see people behind them too. He wondered why Dolf would want to dream about so many people. Sam felt dwarfed by them all and very insignificant. He gazed down at the hall again. It was hard to see whether it was men or women down there. They all wore the same drab overalls. But the longer Sam stared at them, the more he had the urge to go and join them. He would be safe down there, one of the masses. He could be part of them and he would belong. He wouldn't ever have to worry again or make decisions or be responsible. He could join in the exercises and eat his dinner and go to sleep. Was there a way to get down there?

Then, without his permission, his legs were carrying him forward again, along the balustrade to a rusty door, which he found himself pushing open. A flight of marble stairs led down and Sam took them. The soles of his bare feet slapped against the cold stone. He ran, floated, slid down the interminable stairs, wondering if he would ever hit the bottom or if he would be caught here for ever, going down and down, spending eternity descending. No – because now he was running, running swiftly through a large hall. He commanded his legs to stop and it was only with a massive surge of willpower from him that they did so.

Sam found himself in a large, egg-shaped space. Along each side there were curving rows of black marble figures. They were about two metres high and were sitting Egyptian style, ramrod straight. Their faces were oval and each had two holes for eyes and one gaping, screaming hole for a mouth. In between every ten figures a gas lamp flared, casting weird, moving shadows over the floor. Again Sam found himself running. He could make himself brave in his mind, but his legs didn't get the message. They sped faster and faster, so fast that he found himself lifting off the ground. He was flying now, not like in Amy's Dream Kingdom, where he floated pleasurably in the balmy air, but as if he had been fired like a torpedo and was shooting towards a black square in the distance.

The black square was a large metal door, a magnet, and he could feel its pull. He knew that if he did nothing he would smash against it. His arms flailed and his legs kicked, but it was no use. He was being sucked helplessly towards the door. Air shrieked and whistled past him. The door grew larger and larger. Inside his head he shouted silently, 'Amy! Help!'

The door loomed large now and there was no way of avoiding it. Sam shut his eyes, braced for the collision. But it never came. Instead he passed straight through the door and was in a room where a large computer sat on a platform. There was a black leather chair placed at an angle to it. Sam felt the seat and it was warm. Clearly someone had been sitting there and had just left the room. He took a deep breath to try to calm his fear. He knew he might not have much time, so he quickly surveyed the room. It was bare except for a row of filing cabinets. On the computer screen he could see the same hall he had witnessed before, but now all the different groups of people were bowing, all together, thousands of them, to some unseen deity.

Sam got closer to the screen. The picture faded and was replaced by a diagram of a circuit board. Some connections flashed red, some green. On the top of the screen black letters spelled the word: SIMILATOR. Sam stared at it, trying to work out what it could be. Then the scene in the hall returned, obviously some sort of screensaver. To the right of the computer screen were assorted documents.

Sam picked up the top one. It was the rules and regulations for pupil behaviour at Park Place Community School. Below that was a photograph of an Indian gentleman sitting on a bench in a courtyard. Next was a doctor's prescription. But were these things actually in Dolf's Dream Kingdom, or were they objects from Sam's own mind that had appeared there? That was the trouble with dreams. You could never be quite sure about what you were seeing.

But finding things connected with his real life emboldened Sam. He returned his attention to the computer screen and used the egg-shaped mouse to click on a list of recently used files. They had strange names: Scipio, Piers, Gerontius, Sigmund. Sigmund! Sam wondered what the computer had to say about him. He clicked on the name, only to find another circuit diagram, which he could make neither head nor tail of. He frowned in concentration.

He became aware of a cold sensation on his shoulder. Was there a draught somewhere? No, the coldness felt like fingers. Very, very slowly, Sam turned his head to see who or what it was that had placed a hand ever so carefully on his shoulder, sending shafts of ice tingling through his veins. The person was dressed in a black suit, like an undertaker. Sam's eyes travelled upwards.

'Welcome to my Dream Kingdom,' said Dolf.

It was Dolf all right, but there were holes where his eyes should have been.

Chapter Nine

Dolf seemed to be able to see just as well through these two dark hollows. His face was turned towards Sam and his mouth was curved in something like a smile.

'Did you think you could enter my kingdom undetected, Sam?'

Sam said nothing. He felt a burning sensation on the soles of his feet. He lifted one to examine it. A pattern glowed on it, similar to the circuit board on the computer.

'As soon as anyone steps into my Dream Kingdom they are marked,' Dolf said. 'Nothing happens here that is not by my will. And you have come by my express invitation. I intended you to find the egg, the key to my Dream Kingdom. You may wonder why I hid it. You see, I already know you well enough, Sam, to know that you will want to do the things that are most difficult. I tempted you. I knew you would find the key.'

It was hard not to look at the holes that were his eyes. Sam gave in. The dark depths of them seemed to go on for ever. Sam wondered where he kept his real eyes the rest of the time, unless the holes were his real eyes. All very confusing. He dimly noticed that his fear had gone. Here he was talking to Dolf, and it was OK.

'Where do you keep your eyes?' Sam asked.

'Would you like to see?'

'Yes, please.'

'Accompany me down to the great hall, if you will.'

Sam rose and followed in Dolf's wake. As Dolf glided in front of him, he created a kind of vacuum and Sam found he was trapped, floating, within it. It was easy to let go and enjoy the sensation. He drifted through a temple and into the hall. Now he was face to face with the masses of people. There were groups chanting words which echoed through the vast space. Another group were painting a wall, all of them making brush strokes in unison.

'I want to paint,' Sam found himself saying.

'And so you shall,' Dolf replied. 'But first you must eat.'

How kind he is, thought Sam.

His feet were on the floor now and he walked over to a seemingly never-ending queue of people at the canteen. Yet the queue moved quickly as, one by one, each of them was served. Tray held out, scrambled eggs in, tray removed. One, two, three. Sam found a tray in his hand, held it out, received his eggs, took them away. Swept up by the queue, he arrived at a long table, sat down, took a mouthful of egg and found it tasted of sweet and sour sauce. The surprise jolted him and he spat the egg out.

He looked up to see if any of the people

around him had noticed his rudeness. Now he could see that they were not proper people – they were more like shadows. No, not shadows, because he could detect their skeletons beneath their paper-thin skin. They made him think of prisoners, prisoners who had lost the will to fight. Fear seized him again. I've got to run, he thought. He pushed his tray to one side and darted through the tables. The echoing chanting changed now to the unmistakable words, 'Stop him!'

Sam carried on running, but he could tell it was going to be no use. Just as his feet had carried him swiftly to Dolf before, now they were pulling him back. Despite all his effort, he was making only the slowest progress, each stride seeming to take for ever, as if he was wading through sticky treacle. He was being chased behind by thousands of the skeleton creatures. Sooner or later they would get him. And if they didn't, in front of him were hundreds and thousands of them, hundreds and thousands. Hundreds and thousands of every colour, red and blue, green and golden, purple and orange . . . Suddenly the colours were inside Sam's head and exploded with a sharp pain like a migraine. His hand shot to his forehead.

He opened his eyes. All he could see was red. What had happened? There was a red glow everywhere and a taste of sweet and sour sauce in his mouth.

'You're in my Dream Kingdom now,' Amy said. 'Have a swim in the ocean and say hello to the dolphins.'

Amy's Dream Kingdom? How on earth did I get here? Sam thought. Just a moment ago I was in Dolf's world. As he thought that, he saw Dolf's prisoners in his mind's eye and felt them pressing on him. Then the picture in his head began to break up. There was just white noise. He blinked hard and saw that there was no doubt about it – he really was in Amy's Dream Kingdom now. Amy was in front of him, juggling with some chopsticks.

'You were in danger,' Amy said. 'So I sent a hundreds and thousands bomb. And I tried to pull you here.'

Sam didn't understand. He shrugged.

'Why don't you have a swim?' Amy said. 'You look all dusty.'

There was Amy's deep blue sea. Feeling inexpressibly happy now, Sam dived into the warm water and felt the soft, slippery side of a dolphin nudging him. Another sniffed at his feet and seemed to remove something. Sam guessed it was the pattern of the circuit that Dolf had put there. He felt a lot lighter now. He kicked and splashed, knowing that Amy was somewhere by his side. It was all so relaxing and enjoyable. It was like being on holiday when you swam for a while, then came out of the sea and found a deckchair on the beach, then snuggled up in it and let the sun warm you to sleep . . .

But sometimes when you were asleep in a deckchair in the sun, a cloud would arrive from nowhere and it would go cold, and you would shiver and wish you were indoors. And as Sam thought that, a cloud did arrive and he was cold again. He opened his eyes. He was in his own bed and the dream was over. He was facing the wall, curled up tight. Someone was in his room, standing over him. Presumably it was his mother. He knew it was Saturday morning and he had promised to help her at the supermarket.

'Are you all right?' asked Dolf. 'I thought I heard you shouting in your sleep.'

Sam was instantly wide awake. For one dreadful moment he thought he was back in Dolf's Dream Kingdom. But his eyes confirmed he really was in his own room. He didn't have time to think about the dreams he'd just had. Dolf was standing over him. He wondered how he could get away.

'Yes, I'm fine.'

He sat up in bed. Dolf looked quite normal. He was dressed in jeans and a navy sweater. He had eyes, but they'd lost that unnatural flatness. They were normal, brown eyes. Sunlight was pouring in through Sam's bedroom window, and it was probably that which made Dolf's eyes seem ordinary for once.

'Your mother went to the supermarket early and asked me to stay here to look after you.'

'I don't need looking after,' Sam said.

'Ah, but I've made you breakfast,' Dolf said, in a voice intended to be pleasant.

'I'm not hungry,' Sam replied.

'You will be when you see what I've made you.'

Somehow Sam knew that he must not, under any circumstance, eat what Dolf had cooked. Dolf left the room to enable him to get dressed and Sam did so as rapidly as possible. He debated whether to go and find his mum or meet up with his friends. He glanced at his alarm clock – it was already half past eleven. He must have been asleep for ages. He tried to recall his dream but found it had all blurred in his mind and his head hurt when he tried to visualise any of it. So instead he concentrated on washing and getting dressed and going downstairs. Perhaps he would stay in and watch TV. It was good watching TV, knowing all your friends and hundreds and thousands of other people were all watching at the same time. His head throbbed again.

Dolf was in the kitchen, standing by the cooker. 'I've scrambled you some eggs,' he said. 'My own special recipe.'

Just then there was a knock on the door. Both Sam and Dolf turned. Sam ran to see who it was. Outside stood Amy, Dean and Hannah, together with a man in a bright striped pullover.

'This is my uncle Jim,' Hannah said brightly. 'He said he'd take us boating in the park. Come on, Sam, it's late! Get your jacket and let's go.'

'But I haven't had my breakfast yet.'

'He hasn't had his breakfast yet,' Dolf echoed.

'I'll buy him breakfast,' said Hannah's uncle, as Hannah grabbed Sam by the hand and pulled him outside.

'Come on,' she said. 'Run!'

They all fled down the road, even Hannah's uncle Jim. They turned into the main road, ran past Amy's takeaway and didn't stop until they arrived at a little café run by some Italians. Uncle Jim held open the door and they filed in, still panting. There was a large table at back and they all settled down. Uncle Jim went to the counter and bought food and drinks.

'He hasn't asked us what we want,' Sam commented to his friends.

'He *knows*,' Hannah said. 'Because he isn't really my uncle Jim at all. I haven't got an uncle Jim. It's Sigmund. He met us when we were on our way to call on you.'

Sigmund returned with a plate full of hot toast and the correct drinks for all of them. Sam looked around. There were posters of Italy on the walls – of Rome and the Colosseum, of Mount Vesuvius and a range of white-topped mountains called the Dolomites. They looked strangely familiar, although Sam had never been to Italy in his life. He shook his head to dispel the sensation. He saw the lady behind the counter looking at him rather oddly. She was a large, matronly woman in a pale blue housecoat.

Hannah was munching on her toast and Amy was about to help herself to a slice. Dean just watched.

'I'm glad you're safe, Sam,' Sigmund said. 'There were moments last night when you were in mortal danger.'

'The worst bit was being discovered by Dolf,' Sam said. 'Oh, and being chased by Dolf's shadow prisoners.' He found his memories were coming back. 'And then I was about to eat some scrambled eggs, but they tasted of sweet and sour sauce.'

'That was me,' said Amy. 'In my dreams I knew you were in trouble and there's something magical in my sweet and sour sauce.'

'You did well, Amy,' Sigmund said.

Sam punched her on the arm, as a way of saying thank you.

'And you did well too, Sam. I have found out much from what you saw. And it is all as I feared.'

'Do you understand what Dolf is up to, then?' Hannah asked. There was a globule of butter glistening on her chin.

'All too well.' Sigmund cast a glance around him, as if he was worried about being overheard. They all noticed the lady behind the counter was glaring suspiciously at them.

'The shadow people you saw, Sam, they are the dream images of countless people all over the world. You know that some people claim they never dream. It's untrue. Everybody dreams. But those people who say they can't remember their dreams are in truth captives – in Dolf's Dream Kingdom. He has robbed those people of their dreams.'

'Why?' asked Hannah.

'If you control someone's dreams, you can control them. And Dolf wants control, supreme control. Of you, of me, of all of us.'

'Why?' asked Amy.

'He was always the most ambitious of the Dream Guardians. He was impatient with us because he said we never did anything with our powers. He was never satisfied. But in truth, Amy, I cannot answer your question. Who knows why some people turn to evil? Suffice to say, his plans are well under way. That circuit you saw on his computer, Sam, as far as I can make out it's a design for some sort of contraption – the Similator. His idea, I believe, is to use it to make everyone similar to everyone else. People are far easier to control when they are all identical. There is only one mind to read then. It is in Dolf's interest to make everyone think alike and act alike. Individuality is a threat to him.

'I read the papers you found on his desk. He is busily working on this very neighbourhood, bringing all of you under his authority. At Avalon, your mother's workplace, he is already infecting minds. Your mother is at risk, Sam. He is taking objects and altering them with his Similator. He has your prescription, Dean. Dean, have some toast.'

'I'm not hungry,' Dean said. He was repeatedly kicking the leg of the table with the toe of his shoe.

Sigmund raised his eyebrows.

'Scipio, Piers and Gerontius are three other Dream Guardians, brothers of mine. I have not seen them for some time. I fear for them. It would be in Dolf's interest to enlist them, or at least disempower them. I have tried to enter their dreams, but to no avail. This concerns me.'

Sam felt a shiver down his spine, yet still he dared to ask the question that was uppermost in his mind.

'If Dolf does gain control of the world, what will happen?'

'To all intents and purposes, the world as we know it will end. Everyone will be subject to his will.' Sigmund was silent. 'And for that reason, children, I feel you have come as far as you can on this adventure. There is great danger everywhere. And you in particular must take care, Sam. Having been in Dolf's Dream Kingdom, a fraction of you is already under his sway. Do you remember how you felt as if you wanted to join the shadow people and do what they were doing? So take care, Sam. I have no doubt you are of special significance to Dolf, and I think your friends might be too. I need to contact the remaining Dream Guardians and discuss what I have found. Yes, I will consult them, and then together we will attempt to overcome Dolf. I thank you sincerely for the invaluable help you have given.'

Sam was about to protest. As frightened as he was, he did not think he could bear to be shut out from what was to come.

Sigmund lifted his hand and placed it on his own forehead. 'I sense a darkness pressing in on us. These are troubled times. But with strength and resolve, my brethren and I—' His face suddenly contorted in a frightful spasm. 'No, Dolf. You cannot conquer me.'

Sigmund winced again, and Sam was certain that Sigmund could hear Dolf's voice in his head. He found he was gripping the edge of the table. He glanced at his friends. They all looked shocked. Sigmund continued to talk to Dolf's voice.

'I am your elder, Dolf. I can resist you.' He frowned and his forehead furrowed. 'Ah! So that is the Similator.' Now Sigmund tried to turn his head away. Then, as if some invisible hands were controlling his neck, his head moved back and he stared in horror at something in front of him.

'Sigmund?' Sam called out.

Sigmund was looking straight ahead now, with a kind of gawping expression, as if he was watching something in a kind of daze. His lips parted slightly. The pupils of his eyes grew larger. Then he started to whisper urgently.

'Listen – I cannot hold out much longer. Dolf has me prisoner too. Listen. Taste. Taste the elixir. Find it. It will save us all. It can restore us. It is buried, buried – somewhere in the mountains. No, it's at the bottom of the ocean. Or in the desert. I can't tell you – he won't let me

– find the elixir and take it to Dolf's Dream Kingdom. Look after each other. I may not be able to look after you.'

The whispering stopped. Sigmund's head nodded as if he was going to fall asleep. But then he straightened himself.

'I want a cup of tea,' he said, quite loudly. 'Milk, no sugar. And two poached eggs.' He rose from the table and walked in a jerky fashion to the counter, where the Italian owner was looking at him oddly.

'I want a cup of tea,' he said again. 'Milk, no sugar. And two poached eggs.'

The owner glanced at the children. 'Is your father feeling OK?'

'I want a cup of tea,' Sigmund said. 'Milk, no sugar. And two poached eggs.'

Sam didn't know what to do. This was more frightening than any dream. Ought he to call a doctor? Or ring his mum? Before he had time to decide which, or to consult his friends, Sigmund had turned on his heel and was leaving the café. The children watched him walk down the road, head held high, walking almost like a soldier on parade.

Hannah put into words what they were all thinking: 'He's in Dolf's power now.'

The children knew it would be no use to follow him. They got up, pushed their chairs under the table, glanced at the puzzled owner and went out into the street. The cold wind whipped up some dead leaves, which swirled and eddied around them.

'It's up to us now,' Sam said.

'I agree.' Hannah nodded. 'Let's work out what we know. Dolf wanted you to enter his Dream Kingdom, Sam, because that was another way of getting you under his control. He's obviously out to control everyone – either in the real world or in the dream worlds – and he'll try any way he can. And he's getting stronger, otherwise he wouldn't have been able to overpower Sigmund. I don't know why he's so interested in us, though, and Sam in particular. But I think we have no choice except to follow Sigmund's instructions. We must find the elixir, whatever that is,' said Hannah, after a pause. 'He said to look in the desert.'

'And the sea,' Amy added.

Dean just stared at them. Sam saw he had dark rings under his eyes.

'And the mountains,' Sam said, recalling all of Sigmund's words. The mountains . . . *That* was why the poster in the café looked so familiar. They were *his* mountains – the mountains he could see when he climbed the tree tops in his Dream Kingdom. That was where they would start.

'Do you still all have your dolls?' Sam asked his friends.

They nodded.

'I think we're going to need them,' he said.

Chapter Ten

'Are you on your way to bed already?' Sam's mum asked him.

'Yes, but I might read or something,' Sam replied, hoping to throw Dolf off his trail.

His mother was sitting on the settee watching television. Dolf was in the armchair, reading a newspaper. He lowered it for a moment and smiled at Sam. Earlier that day he had thought of telling his mother everything – that the lodger was attempting to get control of his subconscious and was already well on his way to mastering hers. Then he realised how daft he would sound. She would just think he'd been playing a game that had got out of control, and say that there was no reason to be jealous of Dolf. This was a battle he would have to fight without her help. But there was one question he had to ask her.

'Mum,' he said, 'when you go to bed, do you dream?'

'Do you know, it's funny you should ask me that. I used to be such a vivid dreamer, but recently I've been sleeping ever so well. I haven't dreamed at all!'

Dolf's head was hidden behind the paper.

'Good night,' Sam said.

He made his way up to bed and settled himself as quickly as possible. Before he went to his Dream Kingdom there was a lot he needed to think about. Events had been moving quickly, very quickly. Sigmund was under Dolf's control and could help them no longer. They had to find an elixir without knowing what it looked like or exactly what they had to do with it. And they had to outwit Dolf, who seemed to be gaining on them in every direction. Even Sam's mum must be almost under his control. But why did Dolf want his mother? Sam frowned to himself.

The answer popped into his head. Sam would do anything to look after his mother. Wherever Dolf took her, he would have to go. Dolf was using his mother to get at him, he was infecting Sam's own Dream Kingdom and he was attacking his friends. He was even trying to win Sam over by being nice to him. He was trying everything he could. Why, why, why was he trying so hard?

Because . . . came a voice. Sam was still. It wasn't a voice he could hear, but nevertheless the words echoed in his head. *Because* . . . *Because you are* . . . There was a crackling sound. *I will speak again.*

That was Carl, Sam thought. But I don't know who Carl is. Sam wondered if that voice and its half-message were just the beginning of a dream and that he was more tired than he supposed. He tried shutting his eyes. He checked the doll was under his pillow and hoped that Hannah, Amy and Dean were doing the same. He was certain they would be, as there was no time to lose. Tonight they were going to systematically explore the mountains, the sea and the desert to find this elixir.

At first when Sigmund had used the word, Sam wasn't certain what it meant. Hannah had looked it up in the dictionary and told them it was a substance that could change metals into gold or let you live for ever. But it also meant just a medicine. Hannah reckoned it was a medicine that had special powers. Amy asked whether an elixir was liquid or a powder or pills. Dean said his was pills. Sam said he thought an elixir was liquid and he imagined finding it in a little brown bottle or something like that. But the truth was, he didn't have a clue what they would be looking for. And once they found whatever it was they were looking for, then they had to take it to Dolf's Dream Kingdom, all without the aid of Sigmund.

Their task seemed impossible. Yet giving up, Sam thought, was what cowards did. And impossible things did come true. Who would have thought a hundred years ago that a man could land on the moon? Or that you could send an instant message through a computer to someone on the other side of the world? Or that you could travel into someone else's dreams? To help him fall asleep, Sam tried to list to himself all the things he had today that people didn't have a hundred years ago. He reached the vacuum cleaner before he fell asleep.

So it wasn't surprising that when he woke up in his Dream Kingdom he should find a vacuum cleaner. It was working all by itself, hoovering up the multicoloured leaves, leaving in its wake grey, sterile soil. Sam grabbed it to try to turn it off. It snaked out of his grasp and continued its sucking. It was a serpent now, its mouth a nozzle, making greedy, slurping noises.

'Stop it!' Sam shouted.

It slithered away. Sam looked at the

destruction it had left behind. The soil was bare and ugly. He looked at his trees and thought that the branches looked thinner. The leaves gave the impression they couldn't be bothered to hang onto the branches. They weren't gold and red and yellow like in autumn, but pale yellow and washed out. Sam suppressed a shudder. He hoped his friends would turn up soon. The chirping of the greenbirds was weak and thin.

Sam noticed a shape in the sky coming towards him. The red glow around it made him realise it was Amy. She circled a few times and then landed.

'Your Dream Kingdom doesn't look very well today,' she commented.

'How's yours?' Sam asked her.

'It looks all right,' she told him. 'Except every time I ask for ice cream, I get horrible runny scrambled eggs.'

Sam realised that Dolf had a hold in Amy's

kingdom too.

'We must find the others,' Sam said. 'Let's go down to the river.'

In a moment they were there. The river looked different. The water was black in places and a yellow-green fungus was growing on parts of the river bed. Movement in the water suggested that a boat was coming. Soon a barge appeared in the distance. It was covered with a brown awning. Little ripples in the water heralded its approach.

It stopped in front of them, the awning was peeled back and Hannah stepped out.

'Have you noticed,' she said, 'how our dreams seem less like dreams and more real? I'm talking to you and making sense.'

'Yes, I thought that,' Amy replied. 'And also real life seems more like a dream.'

'Where's Dean?' Sam asked.

No one knew. Sam expected he would turn

up in a blaze of noise and activity, but all was quiet. Sam was uneasy.

'Ought we to start without him?' he asked the others. 'Because the mountains are some way away and we only have a night.'

They discussed it briefly before deciding that Dean might appear at any moment and could join them wherever they were. The children then went back a little way into the forest and Sam climbed a tree in order to get a good view of the far-off mountain range. There it was, the peaks shining with bright snow.

'Come and have a look!' he shouted.

The two girls each selected a tree to climb and Sam noticed how Hannah in particular hared up with no difficulty at all. In real life, Hannah was terrible at games and gym. But not in her best friend's Dream Kingdom.

'It's not far,' Amy said. 'Let's fly!'

She took off from the top of her tree and

Sam followed her. He grabbed Hannah's hand and she glided by his side.

'What this reminds me of,' she said, 'is *Peter Pan* – you know, when the children fly to Never-Never Land. I saw *Peter Pan* on the stage once. They did it with wires. You could see the wires. It spoilt it for me.'

Hannah always chatted a lot when she was nervous. Sam thought to himself that flying like this over his kingdom was nothing like a pantomime. Everything looked so beautiful to him. You could believe the land was alive when you saw it below you, the soft curve of greenish hills, meandering streams, cottages nestling in hollows with smoke coming out of the chimneys. Now, though, the land was getting more barren. There were rocky outcrops in the fields. Soon there was just moorland. And in front of them, a solid wall of mountains, rearing up as if from nowhere, barring their way.

A current of air seemed to lift them up and soon they were circling the lower slopes of the mountain range. Gradually they floated down to the ground. There was a rough track that wound up into the mountains, the sort of track you couldn't drive up unless you had a Range Rover. But there was a Range Rover parked close by, so the children got inside and Sam took the wheel. It was a good feeling, being in charge of the vehicle. Sam hadn't realised that he could drive before. It was amazingly easy.

The road curved round and he supposed they were getting higher. He noticed that they passed a wall of sheer rock on their left and a mound of boulders on their right. Sometimes the road opened out and he saw there was a vast drop on one side. Soon, he thought, they would come to the top of the mountains.

'That's funny,' Hannah said. 'I could swear we've passed those boulders before.'

'No,' Sam said.

He drove on along the winding road. There was a wall of sheer rock on his left and a mound of boulders on his right.

'We have been here before!' Hannah exclaimed.

'It's impossible,' Sam said.

He drove on and saw again the wall of rock and the boulders. Hannah was right. They were going in circles. A peculiar feeling like claustrophobia overtook him. Even though they were up high with the eagles and the clouds, they were trapped, going round and round. There was the wall of rock again – here were the boulders.

'I want to get out!' screamed Amy.

Sam put his foot on the brake but to no avail. The Range Rover just carried on, picking up speed. It was far too dangerous to attempt to jump out. They would be going along the mountain road for ever. Suddenly in front of them Sam saw an obstacle

– a landslide of boulders that certainly hadn't been there before. Again he put his foot on the brake. Again there was no response. They were going straight towards it. Time began to move very, very slowly. The landslide loomed larger. There was an almighty crash. Sam found himself in the midst of a mass of twisted metal and a stink of petrol.

'Run!' he shouted.

The three of them raced off, almost deafened by the massive explosion behind them. They ran and ran as the path got increasingly narrower and strange noises boomed and echoed through the air. Sam thought it sounded like laughter. Panting, he slowed down.

'Hannah, Amy, did you hear that?' he asked them.

But they had gone. He shouted their names, even though he knew it was pointless. There was an absence where they should have been. He was alone. He could not go back, as he had come too far. Yet he was petrified of what lay ahead. Every sense alert now, he moved forward. The path dwindled and dwindled and eventually came to a halt in front of a crevasse of jagged red rock. Sam raised his eyes. The sky was a luminous golden blue and he knew if he could get to the top of the mountain he would be safe. It was even possible that the elixir would be there. It was just a matter of scaling the wall in front of him.

He could have sworn he heard the cackle of laughter. Was it behind him? He turned but there was nothing and no one. He found a foothold, raised his right leg so his foot fitted snugly in it, and lifted himself up. The way to climb, he realised, was just to move one arm or leg at a time. He reached with his right arm to an overhang of rock, then found a niche for his left foot and hoisted himself up. It took all of his effort. His body felt as if it weighed a ton. The air was thin in the mountains. Sam also knew that, whatever he did, he mustn't turn and look at the drop behind him. He could hear his own breath rasping. But also he could hear someone else's breath rasping. Had Hannah and Amy come back? So he turned and looked.

Miles and miles of emptiness lay below, dizzying depths of nothingness. He was staring, mesmerised, into a bottomless pit. If he fell, he would go on falling for ever. There wouldn't be enough time left in the world for him to reach the end of his fall. And again, that laughter: a hideous cackle from a diseased throat.

Hot with fear, Sam carried on ascending. His body felt heavier and more clumsy. He missed his footing and slid down a few centimetres. Then he heard his name being called: 'Sam! Sam!' It was Amy's voice.

'Amy!' he shouted with relief.

'I'm behind you!'

He turned again. There was someone behind him all right, but it wasn't Amy. Instead a grinning, jeering demon with green, wrinkled skin and red, blazing eyes stared at him. Lower down were two more figures, also demons. Above him reared the rock. It seemed to go on for ever and ever. Weak with fear and the effort of the climb, and finding it harder and harder to breathe, Sam emitted a wail of hopelessness.

'You thought you could find the elixir in the mountain?' came a voice from what seemed like a little way above him. 'You pathetic excuse for a human being. Not even fully grown, tied to his mother's apron strings! With girls for friends! There is no elixir in the mountains. There is no elixir. You'll have to give in to the master, Sam. Dolf is waiting for you.'

Sam wanted to scream, but all the breath had left his body. He remembered from the real world that if you stopped breathing you died. So he was going to die, then. This must be what death felt like. He tried to take in air but his lungs weren't working. He was suffocating now, everything was darkening and he felt himself falling into an empty, endless grey space.

Chapter Eleven

'Is Sam up yet?' came a woman's voice from downstairs. 'He doesn't usually sleep in this late on a Sunday. Will you check if he's all right?'

'In a moment,' was the reply. 'I'll just finish tidying the lounge.'

'That's kind of you, Dolf.'

Slowly as he came to consciousness, his face buried in the sheets, Sam recognised the voices of his mother and Dolf. He struggled free of the bedclothes and lay there, his heart palpitating. It had been the worst nightmare of all, last night. He could still remember his ascent of the mountains as vividly as if it had really happened. The faces of the demons made him shudder even now. But what had happened to Hannah and Amy? And why had Dean not appeared at all? And as for the elixir, there was no sign of it anywhere. It was hopeless –

he was hopeless. He remembered the cruel, taunting words of the demons.

'Sam?' shouted his mother.

'Yes,' he called back.

'It's past eleven,' she said.

Past eleven, Sunday morning. Normally he'd be up and kicking a ball around with Dean. Now he was lying in bed in a mass of twisted bedclothes. Life was a nightmare. He had better get up and go to call on his friends. Only they would understand what he was going through.

He came downstairs.

'Good morning, Sam,' his mother said. 'Lunch will be at one o'clock. You may do your homework until then. After lunch there will be recreation. Meanwhile, I shall clean the house. Tea will be served at six pm.'

She still looked like his mother but spoke like a robot. Her voice sounded as if someone had recorded it and then played it back for her to mime the words. She was wearing a grey woollen dress with a thin black belt clasping her waist. But what was she saying? He *never* did his homework on Sunday mornings.

'I'll leave my homework till the evening,' Sam said. 'First I'll watch the box, then I'll check out my friends.'

'No, Sam,' his mother said. 'You don't mean the box but the television. And "check out" is a slang expression. You mean you will visit your friends. It's important to speak as everyone else does.'

Dolf entered the room and smiled kindly at Sam. 'That's OK. You don't have to do your homework until the evening.' He put a protective hand on Sam's mum's shoulders. 'Why don't we give your mother some time to herself later on? We could go to the cinema.'

Sam's mum turned and smiled gratefully at Dolf. For a moment each looked tenderly into the other's eyes. Sam hadn't realised things had got this serious. There was no time to lose.

'Well, Sam, will you come with me?'

'I don't know,' Sam said, and switched on the television to block out the sight and sound of Dolf and his mother carrying on together.

It was the news. A lady with blonde hair and a centre parting – who looked exactly like all the other newscasters – was reading the news in the same kind, concerned but rather posh way that all newscasters have. She said a famous burger chain had opened its millionth restaurant in Uzbekistan. There was a picture of it. It looked the same as every other burger restaurant. There was a report from the Paris fashion show. You wouldn't have known it was Paris because, with the traffic, it looked just the same as London and New York and Dubai and Sydney. The report from the fashion show said that this year everyone was going to be wearing workman chic – grey overalls with pockets sewn on the front. A line of vacant-looking models paraded along the catwalk. There was a celebration of something or other in China. Thousands and thousands of people marched through the streets.

So it was happening already. Dolf had begun to exert his influence over all the world. Sam had never realised how much he'd appreciated simple things like being silly, making up his own mind, playing games, giving surprises to his mum, just being himself. All of those things were threatened. Just before, he had been about to give up hope. His nightmare had taken almost all of the fight out of him and had made him doubt himself. But now he realised he couldn't afford to doubt himself. He *had* to find the elixir.

'I'm off out now,' Sam shouted to his mum.

He knocked at Dean's house first. Dean's mum answered the door, looking rather concerned.

'Oh, Sam, I *am* glad to see you! You might

cheer Dean up. His new medicine's working all right, but he's lost his appetite, you know. I can't get him to eat.'

Sam followed her into the living room, where Dean was sitting in an armchair, his eyes fixed on his Gameboy, his thumbs flick-flick-flicking.

'Hey, Dean,' Sam said.

Dean looked up momentarily. There were dark rings under his eyes. 'Oh, hi,' he replied.

His mother stood in the doorway for a moment or two, then decided to leave the boys alone.

'Dean!' Sam said urgently. 'Where were you last night?'

'Last night? I couldn't fall asleep last night.'

'What? You mean, you were up all night long?'

'Yeah.' Dean's eyes strayed back to his Gameboy.

'But we need to find the elixir!' Sam protested.

'Whatever,' Dean said.

There had been times in the past when even Sam had found Dean's non-stop craziness difficult to put up with, but this silent, withdrawn Dean was far, far worse. Was he under Dolf's power? Or maybe . . . maybe it was his medicine.

'Do you think you're not sleeping because of your new medicine? It could be a side-effect. Look, Dean, don't take it any more. Just stop it. Pretend to your mum that you are, but stop it. Throw the pills down the toilet or something. What if the medicine has come from Dolf? Remember, I saw your prescription in his office.'

'Stop taking my pills?'

Sam saw the momentousness of what he was asking Dean to do. If a doctor told you to take medicine, you did. What if it was a life or death matter? But Sam's instinct told him that on this occasion he was right and the doctor was wrong.

'Yes, because you need to sleep and we need you in our dreams. I don't think we can do this without you. Please, Dean. And come out with me now. I want to go and call on Hannah and Amy.'

'All right,' said Dean slowly. 'All right, I will.'

Dean's mum seemed quite pleased that he wanted to go out. The two boys walked over to the Happy Valley and banged on the side door. Amy's dad opened it and then went back to the counter, where he was writing something. Amy ran out and explained.

'He's making alterations to the menu,' she said, her face white. 'He says there's too much choice and it makes problems for him and Mum. So from now on we're only making fish and chips.'

'But you're a Chinese takeaway,' Dean said. 'People expect you to have Chinese food.'

'Mum and Dad say it isn't a good idea to be different.'

Sam and Amy looked at each other significantly. Just then there was another knock on the door and Hannah arrived. All four children were soon sitting in Amy's living room. Amy's mother was hoovering upstairs. She was planning to have a spring-clean, Amy said.

'What happened to you girls last night?' Sam said.

'There was shouting outside my window,' Hannah said. 'I think some people were having a fight. It woke me up. Then I couldn't get back to sleep.'

'I heard shouting too,' Amy said. 'A man and woman. They were swearing and then I heard a police siren.'

'Yes, that's exactly what I heard,' Hannah said.

'No,' Sam interrupted. 'That's impossible. You two live ages away from each other. You couldn't have heard the same fight.'

'Unless Dolf made it up,' Dean said. 'Maybe he wanted to wake them up so they couldn't be with you.'

That was exactly what Sam had been thinking. Quickly he filled them in on his adventure in the mountains.

'But here's an odd thing,' Sam told the others when he had finished. 'Dolf is changing. His eyes are normal now and he smiles all the time. He wants to take me to see a film this afternoon.'

'Don't go,' Amy said. 'It's a trap.'

'I know, but why is he being so nice?'

'*I* think it's another ploy to get you,' said Hannah decisively. 'If he can make you think he's stopped being a danger, you'll be easier to control. Or he's trying to confuse you by being nice one moment and awful the next.' Hannah's brow darkened. 'The girls at school used to do that to me. One day they'd be really friendly and the next they wouldn't talk to me. That was worse, in a way.'

'He's already got my mum,' Sam said.

It was a relief to tell his friends all this, knowing they would take him seriously.

'So he's trying to win over the person you love the most,' Amy said. 'Sam, was your grandmother called Carl?'

'Carl is a man's name,' Dean said.

'Amy, what on earth are you on about?' Sam demanded. He felt a shiver steal through his veins.

Amy gave a shudder and looked around her.

'Amy, you're scaring me,' said Hannah.

'No, it's all right. The ghosts are kind. Sometimes I know there are ghosts around. They come to my house. I haven't told anyone this, ever. There are wisps of them in the air. When I was little there were lots of them but now they don't come so often. But the wisps are here now and I started to think of your grandma, Sam, and I thought she said her name was Carl.'

'I think somebody called Carl was trying to get a message to me in my sleep,' Sam said.

'There are people helping us,' said Amy. 'They're trying to protect us. But they say they can't be with us all the time – it's against the rules.'

Amy's eyes had a faraway look. Sam wondered whether it really was possible that she could understand ghosts. A few weeks ago, he would have laughed at the idea. Now, he wasn't so sure.

'Ask your ghosts,' said Hannah, 'why everyone's so interested in us.'

Amy twitched and closed her eyes for a moment. 'They can't say but they'll try to tell us later at the bottom of the sea.'

'They'll get wet,' said Dean.

'We need to take care,' Amy continued. 'We must all have another dream tonight. We must find the elixir. We must go to the bottom of the sea, like Sigmund said. I want you all to come with me.'

'I like the bottom of the sea,' Dean interjected, sounding a bit more like himself. 'It's got killer seaweed and big ugly fish.'

'Yes,' said Amy.

'I'll be there,' Sam told her. 'But I don't know what to do about this afternoon. I don't want to go to the pictures with Dolf, but I don't want to leave him alone with my mum either.'

'Why don't we all invite ourselves round to your place, Sam, and watch TV?' Hannah suggested.

Sam smiled at her gratefully. He felt safest when he was with his friends. When they were all together, as they were now, he knew he was stronger. The worst bit about last night's nightmare was being alone.

'We'll go back to my house,' Sam said, 'and just hang around until tonight.'

'And then we'll go to the bottom of the sea,' said Dean.

Chapter Twelve

Sam lay in bed, staring at the ceiling. Lying there, he reviewed the events of the afternoon. Dolf hadn't been too pleased when he'd arrived home with his friends in tow, refusing to go to the pictures. Sam's mum had suggested they all went together, but Dolf shook his head. He told Sam's mum the point of going to the cinema was so that he and Sam could bond. Hearing that, Sam was all the more certain the cinema would have been a trap.

Dolf went out after that and, to the best of Sam's knowledge, he had not yet returned. His mother was unusually quiet. She said good night to him in a sad voice. Sam would have stayed up with her, except he had to get to the bottom of the sea as soon as possible. Not only was there the elixir to look for, but there should be an explanation waiting for them.

He hoped that Dean had been able to avoid taking his medicine. He would find out soon enough, in Amy's Dream Kingdom. He was going to see Dean there, at the bottom of the sea. 'Sea' and 'see', thought Sam. They sound the same. So does the letter 'C'. He ran through the alphabet in his head, and then tried to see if he could say it backwards, but he only got as far as 'T'.

On this occasion he was actually conscious of falling asleep. He could feel his conscious mind shrivel until it was as small and hard as a walnut. Then it shattered. His body was weightless. Now he was falling like a leaf from a tree in autumn, dancing in the air, and he landed on a rain puddle under the glow of a red streetlight. He floated on the water, which was as warm as a bath.

Sam looked around him and realised that he had come straight through to Amy's Dream Kingdom. That was convenient, but he couldn't understand why he hadn't started tonight's adventure in his own Dream Kingdom. Suddenly he was gripped by a spasm of anxiety. He knew something was dreadfully wrong. He shouted for Amy. She came running towards him.

'I can't fly!' she sobbed.

'I can't get into my Dream Kingdom,' he told her.

Amy checked her tears to help her friend. 'Why don't we see if we can get there together?'

Sam nodded. They held hands, and felt a current of warm air rush up like a geyser and lift them a metre or two above the ground. Amy kicked hard and she was flying, with Sam by her side, but they were only just above the ground. Sam could feel something pulling at them.

Ahead of them was what looked like a pane of glass. They slowed as they approached it and Sam could see that his Dream Kingdom lay behind it. He ached to get there. He scrabbled furiously at the glass, feeling like his cat, Phoebe, when she was desperate to get in for dinner. The glass remained tough and impassable.

So instead he pressed his nose flat against the glass, screwed up his eyes and peered in. It was his Dream Kingdom, but it was not his Dream Kingdom. There was the forest, but it was bare. Black branches criss-crossed the sky like wires. The greenbirds had vanished. No – they hadn't. He spotted one or two, but they were on the ground, lying stiffly, not moving. Were they dead? Black clouds like the ones in Hannah's nightmare scudded across the sky. He thought he detected a strange smell of stagnant water and decay. Then, in the distance, he saw a column of shadow people marching. His kingdom had been invaded.

'No, no!' he shouted.

Hannah and Dean appeared by his side.

'What's wrong?' Dean asked.

'My Dream Kingdom,' Sam blurted out. 'I haven't got it any more!'

'It's OK,' Dean said. 'You can have mine. It's still all right. I've just come from there. I have a new ride – the Egyptian Chamber of Horrors.'

Hannah cut in. 'There's no time to lose. Amy must take us to the bottom of the sea and, if we can't find anything there, then it's the desert.'

'I'm scared,' Amy said.

'Well, I'm not,' said Hannah. 'I mean, I *am* scared but I'm so used to being scared I feel sort of OK. I can still think straight. Take us to the sea, Amy.'

Amy ran, loping along. The children followed her until they came to the edge of her ocean. The ice cream booth was closed. The waves of the ocean were choppy and disturbed. Sam thought he saw an oil slick in the distance.

'Let's dive in,' Amy said.

They did so. Sam wondered whether they should have provided themselves with oxygen cylinders. He'd read somewhere that if divers are deprived of oxygen they get something called the bends, and it drives them mad. But as they swam lower and lower Sam found he was able to breathe just as well as usual.

As they descended, the water got murkier and murkier. Strange, transparent jellyfish blew puffs of inky black smoke in their direction. They encountered waving, yellow, bubbly seaweed which wrapped itself round their legs and arms, and delivered sharp little stings. Dean fought viciously against the seaweed which had wound itself round him, but it was no use. Until, inspired, he bit into it. It gave an unearthly shriek and shrivelled.

'Eat your seaweed!' he called to the others.

They did so.

'Mine's nice,' Hannah said. 'Like we get at your takeaway, Amy!'

Sam was surprised that they could all talk under the water, so he tried it too.

'Well done, Dean!' he shouted, and discovered that the water was not real water but a kind of thick, damp air.

Eating their seaweed gave the children heart and they swam lower still. They all started as they came face to face with the ugliest fish they had seen in their lives. Its colourless skin was completely transparent, and they could see its organs inside, pulsing away. Its mouth hung open, revealing yellow, crooked teeth. Its vacant eyes stared ahead. Then a shoal of worm-like fish appeared from nowhere and in an instant the children were surrounded by them. Amy shrieked and shrieked. Sam knew she had hated worms ever since a boy in their class had tried to put one down her jumper.

'They'll be gone in a moment,' Sam shouted, hoping to encourage her, but that proved to be a big mistake. Hundreds of the little worm-like things swam into his mouth. He spat and spluttered to get rid of them.

Eventually, as they swam lower, the worms rose above them, until they vanished.

Lower still, and lower. Beneath them were shadows, and Sam wondered whether they had finally reached the bottom of the ocean. Dean was some way ahead of him, and he heard him shout, 'Land!' Soon all the children had their feet on the damp, sandy ocean floor.

'What's that?' Hannah asked. She pointed ahead.

'It looks like some sort of wreck,' Sam said.

The children swam over and found that it was indeed a wreck, of an old galleon, with broken masts and a wooden deck that had caved in in the middle. There were stairs leading down to the lower decks.

'I bet the elixir is here!' Amy exclaimed. 'Because you get buried treasure in shipwrecks and Sigmund said it was buried. We must find a chest and look inside it.'

This made sense to Sam, and all the children agreed that was what they would do. Carefully, holding onto a rail, they descended the wooden steps that led down to the hold. It was dark there, and all Sam could make out were the shadowy shapes of kegs and boxes. As their eyes got accustomed to the light, they saw more. The boxes had writing on in a foreign language. And there, in one corner, was a large chest, tightly chained and padlocked.

Sam approached it and tugged at the chains.

'Maybe the wood is so rotten that if we all tug as hard as we can, we can open the chest.'

They came over and began to pull. It took all their strength. Sam thought, after a few minutes, that he heard a cracking. He shouted to everyone that they should redouble their efforts. The cracking was audible to all the children now. And then, with a mighty creak, the wood splintered and, like jack-in-the-boxes, out sprang three white-masked faces.

'Scipio!' cackled one. His eye sockets were black pits.

'Gerontius!' screeched the second. A trickle of blood glistened at the side of its mouth.

'Piers!' hissed the last, and, as he spoke, they felt a faint, electric shock.

All three of the ghastly faces guffawed at the terrified children.

The first spoke again. 'Do you remember us, Sam? We climbed with you up the mountain. You were scared of us then and you're scared of us now. Your friends will learn what a coward you are. Coward! Coward!'

It was odd. Sam knew he should have been terrified. But the emotion that welled up in him was not fear. It felt white hot and blazing. It sent fire through his veins. He was furious.

'Go!' he cried. 'You have no place in Amy's Dream Kingdom. You're dead. You don't exist. You – are – NOTHING!'

He didn't know where the words had come from, but it hardly mattered. They worked. The skulls fizzed and dissolved in front of Sam's eyes. He had a sense of having done something right. He felt Amy's hand on his arm and heard Dean saying, 'You were ace.'

'Well done, Sam,' echoed Hannah.

'Come on,' Sam said. 'The elixir's not here. I know it. We must get out of the ship!'

He could feel the water around him moving. He guessed that something might be approaching. There was little time to lose. The children struggled through the undersea currents to the stairs and clambered up. The water was now viscous, like oil. Sam felt himself beginning to choke and it reminded him of the sensation he had had on the mountain top. But they all managed to make the deck. The sea was moving wildly now, this way and that, as if it was reacting to an underground earthquake.

Sam felt Hannah clutching him. 'Look,' she said.

Sam did look. So did Dean and Amy. In front of them yawned a dark cavern, framed by a gummy mass that looked like teeth but wasn't. Sam raised his eyes and saw above the mouth, two round eyes.

'It's a giant whale,' Sam said.

And it swallowed them whole.

First there was an overwhelming blackness. Sam was as stiff as a board, scared to reach out and touch anything in case it was the inside of the whale, its heart, maybe, or its stomach. Then suddenly someone switched on a light. Sam found himself inside a circular chamber with panels of lights and switches. There were Hannah, Amy and Dean looking just as bewildered as he was.

'Are we in a whale or what?' Hannah demanded.

'Neither,' came a female voice. It was electronic-sounding, like the ones that answer telephones or make train announcements. 'You are in a Dream Capsule. You have been brought here for your own safety. You will shortly be delivered back to the surface to continue your quest.'

There was a click. The children looked at each other, encouraged but still baffled. Little by little they moved around the chamber, drawn to the walls of switches and dials and buttons. Dean pressed a few. Nothing much happened. Then the chamber darkened and one of the walls began to glow with light. The children watched as a shape formed on it. It was a man's head and shoulders. He had iron-grey hair, steely-blue eyes and regal features.

'Greetings,' came a deep voice. 'I am Carl.'

'Hello, Carl,' Sam said.

'I am also a Dream Guardian. We are diminishing in number. Scipio, Piers and Gerontius have gone over to the other side, to Dolf. Sigmund is held captive by Dolf. All of us are at risk. But we have ascertained why it is that Dolf has concentrated his efforts on overcoming you, Sam, and your friends. It is as Sigmund suspected. Each of you has the gift of Outsight. Outsight is what enables the Dream Guardians to travel through dreams and protect sleepers. We can see beyond our own vision and into the subconscious minds of others. Many children have Outsight, but as they grow the gift may be lost. In others it can be developed. Dream Guardians are generally older people and most are very old. I myself am 223. But you, Sam, and your friends are unusual cases. Your gifts have developed particularly strongly as you care so much for each other. You have taught yourself to feel each other's feelings.'

As Carl spoke those words, Sam recognised their truth. It was his soft side that Carl was talking about. And Amy could see ghosts and Hannah felt too much and Dean – well, there were no limits with Dean.

'And so you pose a very real threat to Dolf. He wishes to control the world. He must either bring you under his sway or destroy you. He is leaving nothing to chance. He is pressing on you in every direction. He is affecting the real world in which you live – he is controlling your mother, Sam. He is invading your own Dream Kingdoms. One way or another, he plans to get you. And he will. Unless you can find the elixir.'

'I don't get it,' said Hannah, biting her nails nervously. 'Just because we have this Outsight, why are we a threat to Dolf?'

'Because if he leaves you all alone, you might become Dream Guardians in time and you would pose a future challenge.'

'Yeah, we'd never let him get away with it!' Dean exclaimed. 'Carl, will we live for ever?'

'No, not for ever. No one lives for ever. Sam, you are in special danger. Dolf believes that, as you have no father, he will be able to overcome your resistance more easily. Show him he is mistaken.'

'I will!' said Sam sturdily.

'And beware. If he wins you over, or destroys you, your friends are ruined too. The four of you are interconnected. Scipio, Piers, Gerontius and Dolf are connected. I too have three special friends. Sigmund is one.'

Sam felt a wave of pity for Carl. Imagine having your best friend under Dolf's control.

'So, Sam, keep your friends about you. Your loyalty to them weakens Dolf's hold over you. You must be brave and think clearly. But, most of all, you must defeat Dolf. If you can do this, you will prove your ability to be a Dream Guardian yourself one day – you and your three companions.'

Now Sam was possessed by two very strong and entirely contradictory feelings. One was a terrible sadness that his normal, everyday life was no more. He could never go back to Park Place and just be Sam Williams. The other was an intense joy, as he recognised what he and his friends were truly meant to be. He was scared and exhilarated all at once. But the strangest thing was, he never once doubted that what Carl said was true.

'Sam,' Carl continued, 'time is running out. Only a short span is allotted to me for communicating with mortals, even mortals with Outsight. Remember this – Sebastian can be trusted. Farewell.'

'Carl!' Hannah called. 'Tell us where the elixir is. What does it look like? We need your help!'

His image on the screen began to fade.

'Carl! Please!' Hannah cried.

'A golden phial with a honey-blue liquor. It is buried in the shade. Ask Thoth. Farewell.'

The image vanished completely. Sam was overcome with frustration. There was so much more he wanted to know.

'Right!' Hannah said. 'We've got to get to

the desert right away. I know what a phial is. It's kind of like a test tube – it's a little glass thingy. I don't know who Thoth is, but we'll find out. We have no time to lose.'

'Wow, Sam,' Dean said. 'We're like superheroes, like Batman or something. We can do anything now.'

'Well, one day, maybe. But we've got to defeat Dolf first,' said Amy.

She grinned at him. Sam did too. He liked seeing Dean back to his old self. Obviously the pills were another of Dolf's traps. Stopping taking them had been the right thing to do.

'Shall we go to the desert now?' asked Hannah.

Suddenly Hannah wasn't there any more. Sam looked around, thinking she was playing a trick. But she had gone, and so had Dean and Amy. Realising that he was alone, without his friends again, sent him cold with fear. Then the capsule began to rock violently, as if it was being shaken. As if he was being shaken.

'Wake up,' said Sam's mother, shaking him by the arm. 'Wake up! It's time for school. It's Monday morning. Everyone must go to school.'

'No!' said Sam, disoriented. He had never woken so abruptly before. 'I have to go to the desert.'

'You've been dreaming,' his mother said. 'There is no desert here. You must come downstairs and eat your boiled egg. You must put on your uniform. You must go to school. Dolf and I have a very important appointment.'

'An appointment?'

'At the town hall at ten o'clock. We are getting married.'

Chapter Thirteen

Now Sam really was wide awake.

'No! You mustn't!' he said.

Sam's mum gave him one of those infuriating looks that adults employ when they secretly think you're incapable of understanding them. Sam leapt out of bed and stood against the door. His mum would have to get past him first. Then he noticed something odd. The light coming into his bedroom window wasn't proper light. It looked grey and old. Even the tree outside looked ashen. He blinked once or twice, but there was no change.

'Mum, what's wrong with the weather?'

'There is nothing wrong with the weather. It is a lovely, sunny day. Every day should be a lovely, sunny day. Now, get out of my way. I have to find a wedding dress.'

Sam reflected that real life had become as mad as his dreams – even more mad, perhaps. How could he save his mother? There was only one thing to do. As she approached him he put his arms round her and hugged her tight. He buried his face in her chest.

'Mum, please don't,' he said. 'Look at me.'

Sam looked up and his eyes bored into hers. Yes, there was that awful blankness there, but also something else. His love for her brought out an answering echo. Something flashed between them. For a moment she was his old mother. Sam kept his gaze steady.

'Mum, for my sake, can you put the wedding off for just one day? Please? Just one day.'

'One day,' she repeated.

'Do not marry Dolf today,' Sam said.

'I won't,' she said.

Sam realised that he was able to hypnotise his mother. Maybe this had something to do with his Outsight. He even smiled to himself as he thought how he would have loved to have the power to hypnotise his mother before now. All those late nights, extra pocket money, trips to the cinema. As he smiled, she smiled. He was heartened, as he knew now she was partly under his control. But it also made him feel very old to think he could tell his mother what to do.

'Just one day,' he said.

She nodded.

Sam swiftly got dressed into his school uniform. Dolf was making breakfast again, and gave Sam a dazzling smile. Refusing breakfast, Sam grabbed his school bag and shot out of the house. Dean was waiting for him on the street. He looked a lot happier.

'I threw my pills down the toilet,' he said. 'What I reckon is, Dolf was using those pills to keep me awake so I couldn't join you. So what I think is, I've probably got special superpowers. Maybe I'm

MosquitoMan or something. Buzzzzzzzzzzzzzzzz!'

Sam said, 'Maybe you are.'

'Yeah, MosquitoMan. And in my kingdom, right, there's something Dolf didn't want me to find, 'cause that's why he kept me out of it. And I think what it is—' the words came tumbling out of him – 'what it is – it's the elixir. The elixir is in my kingdom.'

'No, Dean. Sigmund said it was in the desert.'

'And the desert is in Egypt, isn't it? And in my Dream Kingdom there's the Egyptian Chamber of Horrors. That's where the desert will be.'

Sam wondered whether Dean was right. Maybe he just wanted so badly to be part of the adventure, he was making it up. Then Amy came haring towards them.

'Sam, Dean, have you seen what's going on?' She was white with terror.

'What do you mean?' Sam asked her. 'Do

you mean the weather?'

'Yes, but that's not all. Come here!'

The three of them ran to the main road. There Sam was brought up short. It was as busy as usual, with people walking to the bus stop or driving along the road, but it was drained of colour. Everything was grey, even the buses. And the people. They all walked at precisely the same pace, in a crocodile file. Every car proceeded slowly along the road, equidistant from every other car. There was no birdsong. Instead there was a thrumming noise like a distant drill.

'It's just like Dolf's Dream Kingdom,' Sam said in a hushed voice.

'Is it too late?' Amy asked.

'No,' Sam responded. '*I* still feel like me, and you two seem normal. Shall we go and find Hannah?'

There was no need. She approached them slowly, looking around her in bemusement.

'It's horrible,' she said. 'My parents have turned into robots. It's like living in a machine and not the world.'

'I wish we could go to my Dream Kingdom now,' said Dean.

'I don't think we have time to wait till tonight,' Hannah agreed.

Two policemen came towards them, completely in step with each other.

'Time for school. You ought to be in school,' they said.

The children sped off in the direction of Park Place.

'Stop running!' the policemen ordered. 'Otherwise you will be punished severely!'

The children slowed, and attempted to walk in line. Their school came into view.

The school was grey. The building site had vanished, to be replaced by a large, egg-shaped temple. The pupils of Park Place were walking through the main entrance, two by two. Their uniform was immaculate. Sam and his friends followed them. All the pupils filed into the school hall. Everything had been taken down from the walls. The hall was bare. No lights were on. The head stood ramrod straight behind the lectern on the stage. The teachers stood in a long row down the side of the hall, in full academic dress. Each wore a black cap and black cape. There was no sound except for the tramping of rubber-soled shoes. No muttering, no coughing, nothing. Just a constant tramping. Sam, Dean, Hannah and Amy joined a row and stood in a line next to each other.

'Good morning,' said Mr Pearson, the Head. 'Today's talk is on the subject of obedience. Obedience is of the utmost importance in the twenty-first century. Obedience enables the wheels of society to turn. Obedience to one master ensures harmony and order. Our one master, Adolphus Hunter, MA, DG.

'I will explain to you precisely what I mean by obedience. It is compliance with someone's wishes or orders or acknowledgement of their authority, submission to a law or rule. The origin of the word is Middle English. It derives from Latin via Old French . . .'

The Head delivered his speech in a dull monotone. Sam looked around him. He could see that his classmates were listening in a trance-like state. He wondered if they were being hypnotised. Certainly he himself felt very sleepy. He nudged Dean, who was next to him in the line.

'We can sleep now!' he whispered. 'And visit your kingdom. Pass it on.'

Dean did so. Sam gave in to the tiredness that was sweeping over him. He hoped it was possible to sleep standing up. He remembered his grandad once telling him about the Second World War, and how the troops used to sleep standing up on the train, propped up next to each other. Maybe if he and Dean propped each other up . . .

But it wasn't necessary. Suddenly he was wide awake and dreaming. The other children in the school hall were just shells, shadow-like people with empty eyes. Only he, Dean, Hannah and Amy were alive. Reality and Dolf's Dream Kingdom had become so close they were touching, it seemed. Or maybe he and his friends were asleep and only dreaming. It hardly mattered now.

'My kingdom is outside,' Dean said. 'Come on, everyone! Follow MosquitoMan!'

Nobody paid the children any attention as they sped away. As Sam expected, there was Dean's Dream Kingdom in front of them. This time they were approaching it from the outside. All around it were stone walls with little towers, flying red flags. The red flags cheered Sam. It could be possible that Dolf's influence did not extend into Dean's kingdom. No one had ever been able to control Dean.

They entered through a turnstile. To their left were the dodgems. The cars were driving by themselves, and frequently crashing into each other with a sizzle of electricity and a din of metal. There was a trampoline full of people-size jumping beans bouncing up and down. And in front of them was a large, painted wooden entrance, saying on it *The Egyptian Chamber of Horrors*. All over the front were Egyptian pictures. Sam saw figures with their hands pointed outward, walking that funny sideways walk Egyptians were supposed to have. There was a mummy wrapped in bandages. The pyramids were there, of course, and a huge black cat with staring eyes. And there was sand, miles and miles of it.

The children entered through a gate. There was a booth by the side but no one was there to take their money. A small car was waiting for them and they climbed in, Amy and Hannah in the front, Sam and Dean in the back. With a lurch and a creak, they began their journey.

The Egyptian Chamber of Horrors was at first like any scary ride. They were plunged into the dark and just caught glimpses of tombs and mummies. One of the mummies had glittering green eyes. They looked away. Then they shot through a mass of sticky cobwebs and felt scarab beetles climbing along their arms. All of them started screaming. They entered another area of pitch blackness. When they emerged, they really were in Egypt.

It had to be Egypt. There were the pyramids, only for some reason people were tobogganing down them. The sun beat down in hot waves. A man was squatting, playing on some kind of flute to a vase that Sam had remembered seeing on Dean's mum's mantelpiece, and a snake with emerald eyes emerged. In the distance was a market. If they hadn't been in such a hurry, Sam would have liked to explore it.

'We have to find the desert,' Hannah reminded them.

Just then Sam felt something strike the side of his head. 'Owww!' he exclaimed. He looked around him. On the ground by his feet was a smallish coconut. 'Who did that?' he demanded.

His friends denied responsibility.

Then Hannah exclaimed in pain, followed by Amy. Coconuts came showering down on all of them, and the children had to shield their heads to protect themselves. In between volleys, Sam managed to look up in the direction the missiles were coming from. In a clump of palm trees he saw Dean and several baboons with baskets full of coconuts.

Dean leapt down, followed by the largest of the baboons. Sam had never seen one close up before. It had tiny eyes separated by a long, pointed muzzle. It was a cross between a bear and a dog, he supposed. He wondered whether it barked or roared.

Neither, in fact. It spoke perfectly good English.

'I am Thoth,' he said. 'God of Wisdom.'

Sam thought the Egyptians must be a funny lot to choose a baboon as God of Wisdom.

'We need to find the elixir,' Amy told him. 'Sigmund said we must go into the desert.'

Thoth made a clicking sound with his mouth and the other baboons descended from the trees. Each of the children was picked up by a baboon and slung over its back. It was a very bumpy ride, and Sam could hardly see anything as he was being thrown so much from side to side. But he didn't mind. He had sensed the kindliness of the baboons and for the first time for ages he actually felt safe. Despite the bone-aching ride, he could feel himself relaxing.

The sun's rays became hotter. The trees disappeared. In front of them were nothing but golden sand dunes. Their brightness was almost too much to bear. Sam wished he had his sunglasses with him, and in a moment he found he did. He was thirsty too and discovered a flask hung around his neck. He went to drink from it, but it was empty. He tried to talk to his baboon.

'I need some water,' he said. 'And anyway, I thought camels were the only creatures who travelled in the desert.'

'We are,' said his baboon, who had turned into a camel.

Sam reflected that camels were no more comfortable than baboons. He stared out into the distance. Just quivering golden undulations of sand and a hard bright blue sky that hurt his eyes. There was nothing else. Sam hoped this wasn't a trap. Perhaps Dolf had planned to bring them out here, where they would be lost for ever. He turned his head to look behind him. There was desert there too. And to the left. And to the right. They were surrounded by oceans of sand, everywhere.

'Look!' croaked Amy, pointing ahead.

Sam could see nothing.

'It's the Happy Valley. My mum and dad are there, peeling lychees!'

But they weren't. It was a mirage. The sand and sun were making Amy see things that weren't there.

'I think I can see my bed,' said Hannah. 'There's a huge bottle of cola on the table by it!'

But there wasn't.

Sam was so thirsty he could have cried at the thought of cola.

'There it is!' Dean's voice rasped. 'My oasis! Oasisssssssssssssssss. Bzzzzzzzzz!'

He shot off his camel and flew, like the large insect that he had become, into the distance.

Was there really an oasis in front of them? Sam hoped so. He could see it too and urged his camel on. But now it turned out that the camel was an illusion. There were just himself, Hannah and Amy, crawling on the sand, willing themselves forward to the oasis.

Every muscle ached. As Sam put each of his hands on the sand, it seemed to give way. His throat had seized up completely. Dean's oasis might very well exist, but would he get there alive? At all costs, he must keep moving forward. The sun was too bright now for him to look ahead. Blindly, he groped and scrabbled on the surface of the sand.

He thought, after a long time, that the sand was getting harder. Was it some kind of stiff grass under his fingers? He tried to open his eyes. He was almost there – at the oasis. There were palm trees, deckchairs, an ice cream van, two DJs spinning discs and some dancing baboons. He inched forward painfully. But once he got to the edge of the oasis, his strength returned. He was here at last. He stood upright. Dean ran over to him.

'I've done it,' Dean said. 'I've arrived at my oasis. I've always seen this place. I never thought I could get here. But I've done it!'

Dean was elated. His happiness was so strong Sam felt it pour into him too. He and Dean hugged each other, then fell on the sand and rolled around in a mock fight.

The girls turned up and stopped them. Sam tried his flask again and discovered that it was now full of a thirst-quenching liquid with a lemony-orangey tang. It was still very hot, but there was an inviting palm tree not too far away, extending a cooling shadow over the ground.

'The shade!' exclaimed Hannah. 'That's where the elixir will be!'

The children ran over and began digging with their bare fingers. The sand was soft and gave way easily. As they got deeper, though, it became damper, and they were gouging out wet lumps of sodden sand with their hands.

In fact it was Hannah who found the box. It was oblong and jewel-encrusted, with a design of two cats' eyes on the lid. She undid the catch. Inside was silvery cotton wool. Carefully she removed it, all eyes upon her. Sam prayed for the phial with the elixir to be there. And, yes, as Hannah parted the silvery covering, there it was, a glass capsule, stoppered with rubber. The contents gleamed a honey-blue. Birds sang, monkeys chattered and every living thing around them expressed its joy. Hannah stared at the elixir, awe-struck. After a few moments she wrapped it back up in the cotton wool, replaced it in the box and handed it to Sam.

'You must guard it carefully,' she said.

'I will,' he answered. 'And we must take it straight to Dolf's Dream Kingdom.'

As he uttered those words, the sun dimmed. The joyful noises about them were silent. Just the mere utterance of the evil Dream Guardian's name was enough to strike terror into the oasis.

Amy asked, 'How are we going to get there?'

'I haven't got the foggiest,' replied Sam.

Hannah was the one who liked answering difficult questions.

'OK. I vote we ought to try to wake ourselves up because school was being taken over by Dolf, right? And maybe he's turned school into his Dream Kingdom, so they're one and the same thing? So all we have to do is wake up and then we're there.'

'That almost sounds too easy,' Sam reflected. 'And even if you're right, what do we actually *do* with the elixir once we've arrived?'

'And how do we wake up?' Amy asked. 'I'm trying to wake up now and I can't.'

'What I'm going to do,' Dean said, 'is make Dolf *drink* the elixir and then bash in the Similator!'

'Yes, but how are you going to get to him?' asked Amy.

'Like this!' Dean shouted.

He started running round and round his friends, making all sorts of noises, then occasionally throwing himself on the ground, as if to evade pursuit.

'If we can't wake up,' Hannah said, rolling her eyes at Dean's antics, 'we have to find a way to Dolf's Dream Kingdom through another Dream Kingdom. Last time, Sam found the egg key in my Dream Kingdom, which proves it was easy for Dolf to get to. Since mine is full of nightmares, it's probably the closest of all of ours to Dolf's. I think we all ought to go there.'

Sam smiled at her. Secretly he had been thinking the same thing, but he would never have dared make the suggestion to Hannah. You can't ask someone to confront their worst nightmare, especially your best friend.

'You're a real hero, Hannah,' he told her.

'No,' she said thoughtfully. 'No, I'm not.

But I'll do what I have to, even if I don't like doing it. I never used to be like that.'

'Yes,' said Amy. 'I know how you feel. I never spoke much before to people because I was scared they would think I was different. Now I know it's good to be different, I'm not so scared any more.'

'Bzzzzzzzzzzzzzz,' said Dean. 'Follow me!'

'Come on,' Sam laughed.

After all the serious talk he felt like a bit of fooling around. He started chasing after Dean and called to the girls to join in. Dean ran faster and faster. So fast that the desert seemed to blur and the golden sand lost its shine. So fast that Sam was certain they had left the desert now and were hurtling towards somewhere different. The atmosphere seemed to change. Rather than the crazy happiness of the oasis, Sam felt a dark tension invading him. Fear clutched his chest. He had felt the same sort of fear only very recently. It was when they had all been to Hannah's Nightmare Kingdom. As they continued to run, faster than the wind, Sam knew that Hannah's Nightmare Kingdom was precisely where they were heading.

Chapter Fourteen

Sam, Hannah, Amy and Dean were running through a wide brick tunnel and their combined footsteps gave off a deafening echo like thunderclaps. Sam knew for sure they had arrived in Hannah's Nightmare Kingdom. They all began to slow their pace. As they did, one side of the tunnel vanished and they found they were jogging alongside a railway track. Sam heard the crackle of an approaching electric train. It appeared in a moment, an underground train full of people going to work. It was moving in the same direction as they were going. He could see faces in the windows. He scanned them, looking for someone whom he sensed would be there. And – yes – there she was. He had found his mother. As he had begun to fear, he saw her seated next to Dolf. His eyes locked with his mother's, and he saw her distress and confusion. He had to reach her and get her away.

'My mum's in there!' Sam shouted.

But it was too late. With a whoosh the train had gone. There was no way they could follow it. As they ran on Sam felt rising panic and emptiness. His mum was being dragged away from him. Was she going to be able to keep her promise, or had Dolf taken control of her?

Hannah was in the lead now. They followed her into an abandoned bus terminal where red-eyed rats scuttled sideways like crabs across the ground. Everyone was exhausted after their dash through the tunnel, and each of them sat down on the broken walls and rusting metal benches to catch their breath. None of them said anything. Sam wasn't in the mood for talking. Something was making him feel bad. It might have been his helplessness at not being able to save his mother. He found himself being taken over by a terrible feeling of shame and embarrassment. It was like the time he missed a goal in an important match last year in front of the whole team. It was like when Hannah had once burst into the bathroom in Sam's house when he was using it. It was worse than both of those occasions rolled together. He felt horrible. He didn't want to be with his friends any more. He just wanted to run off and hide somewhere where they couldn't find him.

Gradually he came to his senses. This awful feeling was part of the nightmare. Something had got into his head and was scaring him from the inside. That impulse to run away and hide would be playing right into Dolf's hands. He wanted to separate him from his friends, Sigmund had said. Just realising that helped Sam to fight back and banish his feeling of shame. And then an ancient double-decker bus arrived.

Instead of a driver there was a large, hairy tarantula smoking a pipe. The children got on and tried to run upstairs. One or two of the stairs were missing and they had to clamber carefully over the gaping holes. Wrinkled, papery hands reached from the holes to try to grab their legs. Luckily they were able to kick them away. Once they were upstairs and seated, the bus lurched off.

It took them through a wasteland of abandoned building sites, car demolition yards and factories belching out a vile-smelling, bluey-black smoke. The smoke turned daytime into night. Finally they emerged into the city. The sky was pitch-black now and thunder cracked. Sam heard gunshots and the waah-waah of sirens from police cars, ambulances, fire engines. Up in the sky a sonic boom reverberated. He put his hands over his ears.

He made himself look out of the bus window again. It was smeared with hair grease from countless oily heads. The city looked dirty and menacing. Filthy rivulets trickled in the gutters. Gradually the bus began to go faster. As it picked up speed it shook more and more. The brakes weren't working, Sam feared. The bus careered round a corner and tilted so sharply that he could see the pavement coming up to meet them. If the bus fell over, they would be smashed to smithereens.

But the bus righted itself and carried on. Sam realised that it wasn't going to crash. The point about nightmares wasn't that awful things happened to you, but that you were always thinking they were *going* to happen to you. That was what made up a nightmare. So if you stopped fearing, the nightmare would cease. Sam was on the verge of communicating this discovery to his friends when an image flashed into his mind. He saw his mother walking along their street, arm in arm with Dolf. They were going to the register office. If he didn't get back to reality soon, it would be too late. While he was with his mother, she would be safe, but here in Hannah's Nightmare Kingdom he could do nothing. He understood now that he had lost all influence over his mother. She was entirely in Dolf's control. He had to wake up, otherwise all would be lost.

'I want to wake up!' he shouted.

Hannah's nightmare seemed to fast-forward, and the children were off the bus now and running again. They were being chased by a man with a ray gun. Sam knew if he left his friends they would be shot dead. So before he woke up they had to outrun the gunman. But the harder he ran, the slower his legs became. His muscles wouldn't obey the commands of his brain. Yet his friends didn't seem to be affected in the same way he was. Hannah, Amy and Dean were ahead of him, running swiftly. The gunman was after *him*. That much was clear now. Ought he turn and see who it was, or just run? But running away was what cowards did.

That was why Sam decided to look. He turned, and facing him was the barrel of the ray gun, flashing sparks of fire. A finger was about to press the button. Sam looked up slowly. The hooded figure holding the gun had no features. It was entirely blank. Sam was rooted to the spot. Then Hannah appeared from nowhere and jumped on the gunman. He dissolved into a dirty smear on the pavement.

'Got him,' panted Hannah. 'Now run, Sam!'

Sam did. In between harsh, painful breaths, he told Hannah, 'I've got to get to my mum!'

'Your mum,' Hannah echoed.

'Your mum!' echoed the voices from all the skyscrapers, harsh, mocking voices full of contempt and ridicule. 'Your mum, your mum, your mum!'

Sam was filled with rage and hopelessness. There were too many voices everywhere. There was nothing he could do. More than anything he wanted to wake up, but Amy was right. You couldn't just choose to wake up from a nightmare. That was *why* they were nightmares.

Suddenly, Amy appeared at his side and shouted, 'Watch out!'

Sam swivelled his head round. They were being chased again, this time not by a person, but by a black car, something like a taxi. There were shadowy figures inside. The headlights glared maliciously at him. It drove onto the pavement to get him, cutting him off from his friends. There was nothing Sam could do but run. He was on his own. On his own. The one thing Sigmund had warned him against – being on his own, and he was in Hannah's Nightmare Kingdom. The taxi was chasing him, preparing to mow him down. What could he do now?

He ran on, feeling incapable of drawing another breath. The taxi was gaining on him. Then he saw an alley to the side. He darted down it, pushing over dustbins, which clattered to the ground. He came to a dead end and there was a fire escape. He darted up it. The taxi was at the alley entrance, and had become tall and thin to squeeze itself through. It was still coming for him.

Sam climbed the stairs and at the top he found a door. He pushed at it and it opened. He fell into the building, fell and fell and fell down a bottomless shaft. He heard his mother's voice calling to him, saying, 'I've got to do this, Sam. For you as much as me.' Falling, falling. Until he collapsed in a heap on the school hall floor.

Sam scrambled to his feet. Had anyone noticed that he'd been asleep? Was Dean awake? He tugged at Dean's blazer sleeve. His friend didn't respond. Sam looked at his face and saw that his eyes were glazed over. Hannah and Amy too looked like statues. Sam seemed to be the only person in the whole hall who was capable of movement. He was unsure whether or not to leave his friends but didn't see what good he could do by staying there. Besides, his mother needed him. He left his row and began to walk along the side of the hall, past the zombie-like teachers towards the exit. Once he reached it, he headed straight to the register office.

The walk there gave him a few moments to think. So much had happened in such a short space of time. He had the elixir – that was good. But his friends were still in Hannah's Nightmare Kingdom and he had no way of knowing whether they were OK or not. Hannah had saved him from being shot but hadn't been able to stop that taxi chasing him. He had escaped by falling through a building. But the strange thing was, he didn't feel as if he had escaped. He had this sense that someone was watching him, a feeling that belonged more to Hannah's Nightmare Kingdom than the real world. He wondered whether Dolf had the power to make the real and dream worlds one. Maybe that was what he had been trying to do all along.

Now something clicked in Sam's mind. That was it. Dolf was busy creating pathways between the real world and the dream worlds. That was how he had been able to control all the people in his town. No longer were all the worlds separate.

Anything could happen now.

He wished his friends were with him. He feared he would be powerless without them, as Carl had suggested. But one thing at a time, he told himself. First he must get to his mother and rescue her.

Sam knew where the register office was. It was part of the town hall, a ten-minute walk away – or a five-minute run. He belted off, along his street and on to the main road where grey machines were still plodding up and down. Then he came to the junction, sped over the road and made a right turn towards the town hall. Once he saw the familiar building with its white pillars and semicircle of steps, he increased his pace. It was on the other side of the road to him. He would have to cross.

Who was that getting out of a taxi in front of the town hall? That tall, dark man in a black suit and that woman in a grey dress? It was Dolf and his mother. He had arrived not a moment too soon. He had to hurry.

He threw himself across the road just as the taxi's headlights gleamed ferociously, its engine revved fiercely and it leapt into action. It raced towards Sam. He knew beyond a shadow of doubt that this was the taxi from Hannah's Nightmare Kingdom. It had followed him through the veil between kingdoms, at Dolf's command. Time seemed to slow as the black car came hurtling towards him. Sam was paralysed with fear. Then he felt the thud as the bonnet hit his body and he was thrown up into the air like a football. For a moment he seemed to be suspended above the road, but then he came hurtling down, hitting his head on the side of the kerbstone. There was an explosion of pain and light.

All was silent.

Chapter Fifteen

Everywhere was white and light. The light hurt his head and his body ached too. With a small part of his mind Sam thought that if he *hurt*, then he had to be still alive. But where was he? Could he open his eyes?

Yes, he could. He saw a window, high up, where the light was coming from, and a basin in the corner with a chrome tap. There were machines too. And he was in a bed, and there were things attached to him, and to the left he could see a monitor and it was flashing. Everything felt completely real. This was a hospital room he was in, but he couldn't remember how he'd got there. He seemed to be alone and he wished someone was with him. He wished his mother was with him. But there was some problem about his mother – he couldn't remember what it was.

There were other problems as well. In particular there was something precious that he had to look after. His head hurt and so did his arm, and his back too. The precious thing was . . . was something to do with . . . with . . . electrics. It was too hard to remember, so he shut his eyes.

Beep . . . beep . . . beep. That was the machine by his side. He tried to see if he could turn his head to look at it properly. Maybe it was that machine they had in films that showed you whether you were dead or alive. If it stopped beeping, he would be dead. Sam turned carefully and looked at it. A green line jerked across it. He was feeling sleepy again. A boy's name came into his head, someone he didn't know. Alex. Alex Ear. It sounded like something very important and very precious. Sam felt himself drifting off. The screen with the green line was mesmerising him.

He shut his eyes but he could still see the green line. That was annoying, as he wanted just to rest and go to sleep. The green line was keeping him awake. Then a very odd thing happened. The green line grew bigger and changed itself into a green rope, a thick rope, which wriggled its way towards Sam and wound itself around his body. It hurt, and Sam tried to cry out, but it was no use. A voice in his head whispered, *Take care*. It was the voice of an old lady. It was the voice of his grandmother.

The rope tugged at him and Sam did not have the strength to fight against it. He was being taken out of the hospital room and pulled somewhere else. He guessed he was dreaming again. The rope had been sent by Dolf to capture him. Its rough fibres rubbed against his skin. Air rushed past him, as though he was being dragged up into the sky. He could see nothing, because all around him was a dark fog. But as he was shooting through the air he felt the rope unravel, and as it did, he felt himself falling, falling, as he had before in Hannah's Nightmare Kingdom. Was he going to end up back in the hospital room, in reality, or back in a Dream Kingdom? And whose Dream Kingdom?

He landed on a bed. As soon as he opened his eyes he knew where he was. He was in Dolf's room in his own house. Being in his own house was good, but there was a figure standing by the window, blocking out the light, and that figure was Dolf. Dolf was looking at him, a curious smile on his lips.

'Is this a dream, or is it really happening?' Sam asked.

'Hmm,' replied Dolf. 'That's an interesting question. What do you think?'

Sam sat up. As he did, he realised that he was no longer aching. He also remembered being knocked down by the taxi and ending up in hospital. So if he was no longer hurting, then this must be a dream.

'I'm dreaming this,' Sam said.

'No,' Dolf replied. '*I'm* dreaming this.'

Sam surveyed Dolf's room quickly, to size up his chances of being able to make a run for it. Sam was nearer the door than Dolf was, but in the time it would take him to get off the bed and lunge for the door, Dolf could spring over and stop him. And if this was Dolf's dream, he was in charge.

'I *am* in charge,' said Dolf. 'Well reasoned, Sam. I am very impressed with you. I know that Hannah thinks she's the brains of the outfit, but you're much cleverer than her.'

'That's not true,' Sam said.

'It is and you know it. You have a habit, Sam, of associating with people who are beneath you. That Dean, for a start. A special needs boy. He'll never make anything of himself. And Amy can't communicate with everyday people, only ghosts. Come on, Sam. You're worth a dozen of them.'

'They're my friends,' Sam said.

Dolf lifted his eyebrows in amused contempt. 'Anyway, I'm sure you must be thirsty after your ordeal. Would you like a drink? Something to clear your head?'

As he spoke those words, Sam suddenly felt unbearably thirsty, more thirsty than he had ever felt in his life before. And Dolf was coming towards him with a glass of orange juice with a frosting of ice on the rim. He wanted it more than anything. Then he heard that voice again, the voice like his grandma's. It was louder now. Again it said, *Take care.*

'No,' Sam said, his throat dry and sticky. 'I'm not thirsty.'

Dolf brought the orange juice close to him.

Sam screwed his eyes shut. 'I'm not thirsty,' he said.

The drink vanished, and now Dolf sat on the edge of the bed, next to Sam. Sam noticed that as he did so, the temperature in the room became noticeably colder.

'Sam, Sam, Sam,' he said. 'I wish all this tension between us was over. I know how you must feel, having your mother all to yourself and then me moving in. And of course what's made it worse is that your mother and I have become attached to each other. I do understand, believe me. I think what has happened is that you've been weaving your own fantasies around this situation because you feel powerless to change it. Your mother has heard you talking in your sleep, and she told me you've been imagining you've been talking to Dream Guardians and other nonsense. None of that is true. You just have a very vivid imagination. Nobody can visit each other's dreams. Dreams are nothing. Your mother asked me to have this chat with you. She wants nothing more than for you to accept me, and for us all to be one happy family.'

The atmosphere had changed. Dolf was being kind. Sam wondered if it was true what he was saying – that all his adventures had been purely in his mind. Was he mad? Maybe he was just bitterly jealous of Dolf stealing his mum's affection. Maybe if he gave in to Dolf, all his nightmares would stop. For a moment he was tempted.

'Of course, Sam, I know it's hard for you, accepting me into your life. I can never replace your own father. I don't expect to. I just want to be a friend to you. I don't ever want to get in the way of the special relationship you have with your mother. That would be wrong.

'Maybe in the beginning I was a little distant with you. I've never known any boys before and I didn't want to get off on the wrong foot. I've noticed you've been looking troubled. I know you've been having bad dreams about me. The subconscious can play strange tricks. You may have been imagining all sorts of things about me. But I'm just a normal guy, in love with your mother. We're going to get married.

'After the wedding, we've decided you can come away with us on the honeymoon. Where shall we go? Your mother has told me you've always wanted to go to Florida. Well, Florida it shall be, then.' Dolf smiled at him.

Sam couldn't help but smile back. He had been wrong to suspect Dolf. It was childish, thinking this man was some sort of supernatural villain. He would grow up and go to Florida. In fact, his life would be so much better if he had a father.

'Am I dreaming this?' Sam asked again. He had forgotten whether this was supposed to be a dream or not.

'No,' Dolf answered. 'This is not a dream. This is reality. I am marrying your mother and you will be the witness at the wedding. Come downstairs with me now. Your mother is waiting. Kiss her and make up. Let's be one happy family.'

One happy family. That was what Sam wanted most of all. He smiled at Dolf, Dolf smiled back and put a friendly hand on Sam's shoulder. He suddenly had an urge to bury his face in Dolf's chest and let this kind, fatherly man take over. Just before he did, he noticed something out of the corner of his eye. It was a box on the table near the window. It was a jewel-encrusted box with two cats' eyes on the lid. It looked kind of familiar.

'But first, Sam, I want you to tell me something. Say you trust me. Say you belong to me. Speak those words. *I belong to you, Dolf.*'

Yes, he would speak those words and all his troubles would be over. 'I . . . belong . . . to – Oww!!!'

Something sharp jabbed Sam's neck. It stung badly and stopped him in his tracks. He rubbed his neck. He could hear a buzzing. 'There's an insect in here,' he told Dolf. 'A mosquito.'

Dolf looked round, puzzled.

Then Sam heard a voice in his head. It was Hannah's voice. 'Get out!' she shouted.

Then flames licked under the door, which burst open to reveal a Chinese dragon, all green scales and blazing eyes. It roared and Sam stepped back, terrified. It advanced towards Dolf.

Hannah's voice came again. 'Get the elixir! It's on the sideboard.'

The elixir! That was what it was. Suddenly a torrent of memories poured into Sam's consciousness. The oasis, the box, Sigmund's kindly face, his mission to save the shadow people in Dolf's Dream Kingdom. He had to stick by his friends. The dragon looked fearsome but Sam recognised it – it had come from the calendar in the kitchen from the Happy Valley Takeaway.

'It's me, silly,' said the dragon, who was really Amy.

Sam grabbed the box and ran out of the door. There was still a buzzing in his ears, and it was good to know he was being accompanied by Dean the MosquitoMan. He clasped the box close to his chest.

The buzzing was louder now. It deafened him and wiped out everything from his head. Once again he was falling, and as he fell, he thought, I have been dreaming again. But it is all right. My friends were with me. In a moment I shall wake up and I shall be back in the hospital. With the elixir.

He grimaced as he opened his eyes.

'Sam!' said his mother. 'You're awake!' She was smiling at him and crying both at the same time. Her hand reached out and smoothed his hair.

'What happened to me?' he asked her.

'You were running across the road because you were late for the wedding and our taxi knocked you over. But you're all right now. Dolf saved you.'

'Where is he?' Sam asked.

'He's gone back home for a rest.'

'Did you get married?'

'No, darling. We came with you to the hospital. But the nurse says you're going to be all right. You've had concussion and you're badly bruised. I've been sitting with you. You were very restless in your sleep.'

'I was having a bad dream,' Sam said.

He could feel an object in his bed. He wriggled his hand down under the bedclothes and it was as he hoped – it was a box, jewel-encrusted. He had brought the elixir back with him. There was still a chance. He needed to get back to sleep again as soon as possible.

'Mum,' he asked. 'What time is it?'

His mother consulted her watch. 'Seven o'clock. You've been drifting in and out of consciousness all day. Your friends called to see you after school, and they sat with you for a bit, but do you know, they fell asleep here in the ward! I sent them home.'

Then the door of Sam's room opened and a nurse appeared. She looked rather fearsome. She was a large lady with her hair scraped back in a little bun. She had a no-nonsense air about her.

'As I told you, Mrs Williams, Sam will be fine. It's important that you both get some rest now.'

Sam's mother looked anxious. 'I was wondering, nurse, if I could stay the night?'

'Sorry, out of the question, Mrs Williams. Hospital regulations. And besides, you must rest too. I shall look after Sam for you. Come on now. Chop, chop!'

Sam's mother obediently got up, bent over Sam and gave him a brief kiss on his forehead. Sam knew his time had almost run out. He had to deal with Dolf tonight, before his mother had the chance to get back to the register office. He watched his mother turn and leave the room and heard her footsteps retreat down the corridor.

The nurse approached his bedside. She wore a starched white housecoat with a little badge with her name on. Nurse Sebastian, it read. Something clicked in Sam's mind. Carl – he had said that Sam could trust Sebastian. Sebastian wasn't a man, it was the surname of a woman and she was his nurse!

Nurse Sebastian didn't look so fearsome any more. In fact Sam didn't know how he could have thought she was. Her eyes were blue as a summer's sky and her smile was calm and assured. She placed a cool hand on Sam's brow.

'You're doing well,' she said. 'But you are still in danger.'

'I know,' Sam said. 'And so is my mother. But it's OK. Look – I have the elixir.' He pulled at the sheet that was tucked in by his side to reveal the box.

Nurse Sebastian was delighted. 'Do you know what to do with that?'

'No,' Sam said. 'Please tell me.'

'Take it to Dolf's Dream Kingdom. It has the power to destroy the Similator. You must also splash some in Dolf's eyes. But Sam, you must beware. Dolf has tried to win you over, to take you to his side. You have resisted and for the last time. Now his only way of dealing with the threat you pose is by your destruction. You must destroy him first.'

'But how do I get to Dolf's Dream Kingdom?'

'I can help you,' said Nurse Sebastian. 'While Carl was concentrating on aiding you and your friends, I have been working on ways of gaining entry to Dolf's kingdom. I am highly qualified in the pharmaceutical arts. I shall give you two potions tonight. One is a sleeping draught from the hospital pharmacy; the other is a concoction of my own. I have given some to your friends too. Combined with your Outsight, it will enable you to enter any Dream Kingdom you choose, including Dolf's.'

'You can trust me,' said Sam, trying to sound braver than he felt.

'I know I can,' said Nurse Sebastian. 'Carl told me how special you all are. But first it's my duty to look after your real body. Would you like some fresh orange juice?'

'I'd love some.'

As if from nowhere, the nurse produced a glass. Sam drank the juice greedily. It quenched his thirst and made him feel strong again and ready for anything.

'Shall I go to sleep now?' Sam asked.

'No, not yet. You must rest a bit in the real world. I'll get you some magazines. I could bring you a television, but you'd find it depressing. Dolf's influence is too apparent everywhere. Even the soap operas all have the same storylines.'

She smiled at him and Sam didn't know whether she was teasing or not.

Time passed slowly despite the magazines, but when the square of light in the window frame above his bed darkened, Nurse Sebastian came over with her two preparations. She helped prop Sam up in bed so he could drink them.

'I shall see you in the morning,' she said to him as she dimmed the lights in his room. Sam realised that she was being optimistic. There was every chance he might not return. If Dolf wanted his destruction and was successful . . . But he would not think that way. Instead he snuggled into bed and tried to imagine himself scoring a winning goal for City in the cup final.

He shut his eyes, and so began the longest night of his life.

Chapter Sixteen

Sam found himself beside a canal. He knew it was a canal and not a river because it was dead straight. It was rank-smelling and frothy. He stepped back away from the water and instinctively sought shelter. A few yards on his left was a wide bridge that spanned the canal and he dashed under there. The bridge was made of a dull grey concrete. Everywhere was the same grey light that he remembered invading Park Place. He guessed he had arrived in Dolf's Dream Kingdom.

He was definitely dreaming. He knew this because he was no longer in his hospital gown, but in tracksuit bottoms and a hooded top. The box was with him. It looked far too conspicuous to Sam, so, checking he was alone, he opened it and removed the phial with the elixir. It shimmered with a golden radiance that seemed to bring life to the wasteland he was in. It comforted Sam to look at it. But mindful of the task ahead, he put the phial in the zipped pocket of his tracksuit bottoms.

He was pleased to notice he was able to think clearly. This would make his job easier. He wondered if the potion Nurse Sebastian had given him helped him to overcome the powerlessness he felt in other people's Dream Kingdoms. He was alert now and ready for action. He knew he had to find Dolf's headquarters and the Similator – and Dolf.

He peered around him. Since the canal was slightly lower than the surrounding ground, he couldn't really see the lie of the land. He wondered if it would be safe to clamber up the bank to look round. Safe or not, he decided he had no choice.

There was no one about. All he could see was a deserted, flat landscape, relieved on the horizon by a forest of tall factory chimneys emitting wisps of smoke that rose vertically. He didn't remember them from last time. He turned, but the view ahead of him was shrouded in mist. He wished his friends were with him, especially Hannah, as she always had good ideas. Then he heard a rumbling.

At first he thought it was an earth tremor. But soon he realised that it was the tramp of feet. The tramping was fast and getting louder, and it was coming from the direction of the factory chimneys. Then Sam saw a storm of dust, and out of the dust emerged columns and columns of shadow people. They were coming straight for him. Running did not seem to be an option; hiding felt better. Did he have time to get under the bridge again?

No, because now he was being swamped by them, hundreds and hundreds of shadow people. But they did not seem to notice him or want him. Their eyes were dead. Their minds were absent. They were just grey shells of people, their collective stare fixed in the far distance. So many, thought Sam. Dolf had destroyed so many. They were not after him, but he was in great danger of being trampled alive if he didn't take action.

Then a thought came into his head which almost sounded as if Hannah had put it there. *Go with them*, said the voice. *They can camouflage you. I bet they're going to the headquarters.*

It was a good idea. It was Sam's best chance of arriving there undetected. The shadow people had no eyes to see. So Sam twisted round and began half-walking, half-running, to keep up with his strange escort. It was hard work. He was puffing and panting. He noticed that noises were being emitted by the shadow people too. Occasionally he would hear a short sigh. The next time he did, he glanced up at the person it came from. Sam almost thought for a moment it was Mr Pearson, the Head of Park Place. Or had he imagined that?

They marched on interminably, and Sam thought their throng seemed to be increased by the arrival of other columns of shadow people, like tributary streams to a vast river. Eventually they seemed to be marching along a broad highway. Since most of the shadow people were taller than him, Sam still couldn't see where he was heading to. But the darkening sky assured him they couldn't be too far away from Dolf's headquarters. And soon Sam saw that he was walking under a vast archway into a courtyard.

The shadow people stopped. Sam could see nothing, so he tried to squeeze through the gaps between bodies to get to the outside of the crowd. It took for ever, but luckily no one seemed to notice or care what he was doing. Eventually he forced himself between two overalled figures and arrived at a black marble wall, icy cold to the touch. Then with one accord all the figures bowed. Caught by surprise, Sam did not.

He was in a huge walled enclosure. In front of him was Dolf's temple and on a gallery high up was a small, black-draped figure which Sam knew was Dolf. The shadow people were bowing to their master. Quickly he lowered his head, then stood upright again when everyone else did. The mass of people began to chant. Sam couldn't make out all the words, but it was something to do with allegiance and masters and doing someone's will. But by that time he was feeling his way along the marble wall, hoping to find a way in. To his relief, he came upon a door, tried it and found it was open. He entered the building and, as he did so, someone grabbed him by the arm.

'Sam! We made it!' said Dean.

Amy flashed the torch she was carrying around the chamber they were standing in.

'That Nurse Sebastian told us what to do,' Hannah said. 'She said we had to use our dolls tonight to dream with you. She said if you got to

Dolf's kingdom, we would arrive there too. She said you would need help.'

'I brought you this,' Dean said. He was holding out a water pistol Sam remembered they used to play with years ago. Amy shone the torch on it. There were tooth marks on the handle where Dean had chewed it.

'Thanks, Dean,' Sam said. 'I'm sure it will come in useful.'

Amy made her torch dance over the walls. They were a gleaming jet black, like the skin of a beetle.

'I'm looking for an exit,' she said.

'Did Nurse Sebastian talk to you?' Hannah asked Sam.

'Yes,' he replied. 'I've got to pour some elixir on the Similator and splash some in Dolf's eyes.'

Hannah was thoughtful. 'What if you break the phial? Then we're lost. You know what I think we ought to do. We ought to put the elixir in

Dean's water pistol because that's plastic and it won't break.'

Sam wished he'd thought of that.

'Well, all right, but we must do it very carefully.'

'I'll do it,' said Hannah. 'It's only like science, when you fill a test tube, and I like science.'

Sam handed both the elixir and the pistol to Hannah. Very, very carefully, she unstoppered the phial and trickled the honey-blue liquid into the barrel of the water pistol. As she did so Amy was able to save the batteries on her torch because the light the elixir emitted illuminated the whole chamber. To the children's surprise, the old water pistol began to change. The tooth marks vanished and the dull green plastic casing shone emerald.

'Wow!' Dean said, speaking for them all.

Sam put the pistol in his pocket, together with the phial.

Amy began to explore with her torch again.

'I thought I saw something,' she muttered. 'Yes – here!'

The children followed the beam of the torch to where it shone on a low door. They all went over and Sam tried to open it. Again it gave easily. In front of them were metal steps leading down.

'I think that's the only way out of here,' Hannah said.

'Well, let's go,' Sam said.

He led his friends down the stairs. As they descended, an awful stench greeted them.

'Yeuch!' Dean said. 'It smells like a toilet down here.'

Sam thought it did too, and wondered whether they might have arrived at the sewers. He was almost certain he was right when the stairs ended at the entrance to a low, long tunnel, with trickles of slimy water at the bottom.

'Shall we go on?' he asked his friends.

'You tell us, Sam,' Hannah said.

Sam thought. His mind was blank. But something else stirred in him – a feeling. The feeling told him he was near the end of his journey and they were going in the right direction.

'Let's carry on,' he shouted.

His voice echoed in the tunnel. Amy handed him her torch. He used it to help them stay out of the foul-smelling liquid that ran at the bottom of the tunnel. Sam decided they couldn't be in a sewer as Dream Kingdoms didn't need sewers. Nevertheless the murky, thick liquid revolted him and he trod very carefully.

'Sam,' said Amy, 'I think the tunnel's getting narrower.'

Sam thought she might be right. Ahead of them the tunnel seemed to taper. The walls on either side were closer together and the liquid was deeper. Soon it became impossible to avoid stepping in it. In a few moments they were able to reach out and touch both walls at the same time. The surface was rough and bristling with a strange sort of mould. Now they had to bend their heads, and at last Sam decided it would be better to crawl.

'I think we should stop,' Hannah said.

But Sam was already edging forward.

'No,' he shouted. 'I can see something at the end of the tunnel.'

He was certain there was some kind of empty space. He squeezed his way through and, to his relief, emerged into a bright chamber. This one, however, was entirely white. The walls were of white tiles and everything was lit by strip-lighting. In front of him were three doors.

One by one his friends joined him. They were all relieved to be out of the tunnel.

'Which way now?' asked Amy.

Once again Sam felt it was up to him to make the decisions.

'This one,' he said, choosing the middle door.

He opened it and it led to a white corridor. The children marched along it, noticing how it curved round. They walked for ages and reached another door. Again Sam opened it. They were back in the chamber of the three doors.

'It was the wrong one,' admitted Sam.

This time they tried the door on the right. Again they entered a white, curving corridor. This time they ran, not wanting to waste time if they were wrong. And they *were* wrong.

'Let's try this one,' said Dean, tugging at the last door handle.

This time they followed him. Again, a curving white corridor. Again they re-emerged into the same chamber. But this time Sam heard something. It was the same demonic laughter that had tormented him on the mountain. The back of his neck pricked with fear.

'Someone's laughing,' Amy said.

But it was not some*one* – there was laughter

all around them. Sam guessed they were being watched, and it was possible that ever since they had entered Dolf's Dream Kingdom they had been spied on. The tunnel, the corridors, they were all traps. What if his instinct had betrayed him completely?

Once more Sam and his friends found themselves running back to the chamber in which they'd arrived. But this time they were not alone.

Three hooded, white-cloaked figures stood there.

Because they were swathed in white from head to toe, for a moment Sam was puzzled. But when they began to laugh, he knew exactly who they were. They were Scipio, Gerontius and Piers. The children were rooted to the spot with fear.

'Welcome,' said the figure on the right, throwing back his hood and revealing a grinning, toothless face. 'I am Scipio. My brothers and I live here now.'

Sam was silent. He could feel his heart thumping in his chest. They were trapped, he knew it.

'You are all fools,' Scipio continued. 'And you in particular, Sam. Dolf gave you a chance to join him. You could have submitted, as we have done. You could have enjoyed the power we enjoy. Everyone would have done exactly as you said. We are the lords of all we survey.'

'Not of us, you're not!' Dean interjected.

Sam was horrified. But Scipio just laughed again.

'Dolf gave you a chance, but you turned him down. So now he has no option but to destroy you all. That will be relatively simple, as in destroying one, all will be destroyed. If one of you dies, the bonds between you weaken and the others will lose their Outsight. Then it will be a simple matter for our master to control them. So which of you will it be?'

The figure on the left said, 'We should toss a coin. Or throw a die.'

'There's a better way than that, Piers,' spoke the third figure, doffing his hood to reveal a scaly and pitted face. 'Ask them to vote. Ask each of them which one of their friends they would like to die.'

That decided Sam. Until that point he was all for them resisting the corrupt Dream Guardians. But he knew that if one of them was to betray another, they would all be lost.

'Me,' Sam said. 'You can kill me.'

His friends cried out in protest.

'That is quite suitable,' Scipio said. 'You must be sent straight to Dolf. Myself, Piers and Gerontius will look after the others. Perhaps they would like a tour of our menagerie. We have an astonishing collection of reptiles not a moment away from here.'

Sam swivelled round to look at his friends. Too late. They were no longer there. Or rather, what *was* there was a sort of 3D-photograph of each of them. Their real bodies had disappeared. Their images were frozen in time. And the three hooded figures had vanished. Once more Sam was alone.

'No, not alone,' said a voice.

Through one of the doors came Dolf.

Once again he had holes where his eyes should have been. He glided towards Sam and put an icy hand on his shoulders. His voice was sepulchral.

'You had your chance,' Dolf said. 'You could have chosen to come to my side. But you are young and silly, Sam. You gambled and now you have lost. While you are alive and continue to resist me, I cannot achieve full power. You are a thorn in my side. And so I must destroy you.'

'I bet you can't,' Sam challenged him, bold because he felt desperate. 'Otherwise you would have killed me before.'

'I nearly did, on several occasions. But I held back. Would you like to know why? Because you would have been more use to me alive. With your powers, and your friends' powers, who knows what new dimensions and ages we could have conquered? And with you as my heirs – my *heirs* . . . Think, Sam, what you have lost. My reign could have gone on for ever.'

'You're mad,' Sam shouted.

'No, it was the other Dream Guardians who were mad. Sigmund was mad. Look, Sam. Can you see Sigmund now?'

He could. Dolf had imprinted in his mind's eye a film of Sigmund. He was in a dirty cell, with lines of insects climbing the walls. He was dressed in rags and two shadow-people prison warders were standing over him, with whips and clubs.

'Sigmund was mad to mock me. We had a council. I told them that the Dream Guardians were losing their power in the world. I said the way to get it back was to dominate everyone, control their waking hours as well as their dream hours. They scoffed at me and threatened me with expulsion. So I barred them from my dreams and decided to save the world in my own way. And I have come far. You will not spoil it, Sam.'

'You can't kill me,' Sam protested. 'Because I'm not really here. The real me is in hospital.'

'Then I shall kill you in the hospital. That is where the final act will happen.'

'You can't do it!'

'Oh, yes, I can. You underestimate the power of evil, Sam. Grow up a little. Not all stories have happy endings, you know.'

Sam felt his knees give way and he sank to the floor.

Chapter Seventeen

Dolf was dressed in a loose-fitting black suit. From his jacket pocket he took out from a case his pair of blue-tinted glasses. His movements were leisurely. He looked as if he had all the time in the world. Which, Sam thought, in a way he did. Sam surveyed the chamber quickly, just in case a way out had appeared. But the three doors had vanished now. He was enclosed with Dolf for ever.

Dolf put on his glasses and, as he did so, the room seemed to judder. Then Sam's ears were pierced by a high-pitched note at a frequency which sounded as if it could shatter glass. Sam thought his eardrums would explode. He put his hands over his ears and screwed his eyes shut. The chamber vibrated rapidly. Dolf's image seemed to be imprinted on his retina.

When Sam opened his eyes, he was back in

hospital. It was OK. He was in his bed. A soft lamp shone in his room. A comforting line of light came through the bottom of the door. Once again, he had been dreaming. Dolf's threats were part of a nightmare, no more than that. As Sam stretched his limbs and felt the bedclothes reassuringly snug around him, he heard footsteps. The nurse was approaching. The door opened and in came Dolf in his black suit.

'Hello, Sam,' he said. 'I thought I'd come and wish you good night.'

In less than a moment Dolf had locked the door and was standing over Sam's bed. He was still wearing his blue-tinted glasses. He removed them now. He had his old eyes, the flat yellow ones, the ones that enabled him to see in this world. This was the lodger Dolf, but he was also the Dolf of his nightmare, Sam's enemy and his would-be destroyer.

'So we meet again,' Dolf commented drily.

'It was foolish of Nurse Sebastian to go for her break. She can't care much about you, Sam.'

Sam was paralysed with fear. His mind had seized up. He couldn't decide what action to take. He thought it might be best to keep watching Dolf. If he could guess what Dolf was going to do next, maybe he could outwit him. But Dolf did nothing. He stood there, completely immobile. Sam was baffled.

He looked at Dolf's face to see if he could read from his expression what he was going to do. He saw that Dolf's eyes were locked on his. Just like when Dolf had first come to his home and tried to break into his head, Sam found he could not take his eyes away. Each time he tried to shut his eyes, his eyelids sprang open. He could not turn his neck. Dolf's yellow eyes glinted and blinded him. Now they were no longer gold but pitch black, like two never-ending tunnels, and Sam felt himself being sucked towards them. With all his power he tried to resist.

'Don't struggle,' Dolf said. 'It will be worse for you.'

More than anything Sam wished he was back in his dream, safe in the white chamber where Dolf could not harm his real-life body. Back in the chamber, he might be able to escape from Dolf's magnetic, deathly stare. Sam decided to concentrate on seeing the chamber in his mind's eye. It came into view. He wished more than anything that he was there. All of a sudden there was a shriek as he breached Dolf's Dream Kingdom. Now he really *was* back in the white chamber. At least, it seemed like the white chamber, but the three doors had gone. It was also smaller than Sam had remembered it and square. Maybe it was another room altogether. Dolf's Dream Kingdom was very large and it had many chambers. This one he was in was the same size as a telephone box. He heard Dolf's voice speaking to him in his head.

'A clever trick, Sam. Your powers are considerable. But it is too late to escape. I will make you come back to me of your own free will.'

Sam felt his heart thudding in his chest like a hammer. So all he had to do was to stay here. That was all right. He would just not go back to his hospital bed. Until the danger was past, he would stay here. He would be safe. He was playing a cat and mouse game with Dolf – Dolf was the cat and he was the mouse. Mice were smaller, swifter and nimbler than cats. He wiped the sweat from his brow. He tried to relax and breathe properly. He took half a step back and leaned against the white, tiled wall of the chamber. The chill of the cold floor travelled up through his bare feet.

'There's little to do here,' Dolf's voice commented. 'Let me entertain you.'

Now a film played inside Sam's head. This time it was not of the captive Sigmund, but he could see Hannah, Amy and Dean. They were chained together. Scipio, Piers and Gerontius were with them. At one end of the room they were in was a large glass tank, full of hissing, writhing snakes. Sam could even see their little forked tongues darting out. Some shadow people entered then with three chairs and some wooden steps. They placed the three chairs on the glass top of the tank of snakes. They put the steps by the side.

Sam watched in horror as Gerontius prodded his friends in the direction of the tank. They wouldn't move. Then the three demons frogmarched them over to the tank. Dean fell deliberately, which caused some chaos, but Scipio lifted him and carried him, struggling. The others were dragged in his wake. Eventually each child was seated and then strapped into a chair.

Sam heard Scipio's voice. 'At the moment Dolf destroys Sam, you will become shadow people. Should Dolf delay in Sam's destruction, we wish to take no risks. We would be forgiven if we were to destroy you ourselves. If the fancy takes us, we can disintegrate the chairs and the lid of the tank, and you can join our pets in their tank. But beware, they do bite. And although we are fond of them, you will find the touch of their hot skins loathsome. That boa constrictor, Dean, is much bigger than you.'

Sam saw that Hannah was crying. Amy was as white as a sheet. Dean's eyes were screwed shut.

'What shall we do with them, Piers? Gerontius? What shall we do?' Scipio cackled.

Then the picture broke up. Sam began to push at the walls of the white box he was in, desperate to get out and help his friends. It was pointless, he knew, but he couldn't bear to watch them suffer. Yet as he banged with his fists on the tiled wall, he noticed something odd, or thought he did. The chamber was shrinking. He thought he could see the walls and ceiling moving in on him. As he pushed against them, they seemed to be pushing against him. He found himself panting as there was less and less air to breathe. The chamber was no longer a room, but more like a white coffin. In a moment the walls would be pressing against his chest. Already the ceiling was touching his head. The walls were constricting his arms now. Would it be possible for him to escape at all? What if he was to wish himself back to the hospital bed? But there Dolf lay in wait. No, he would have to stay here and hope against hope that the room would cease moving in on him. Maybe if he didn't resist, it would stop attacking him. Sam tried staying completely still, but it was no use: the walls and ceiling continued to squeeze him. The ceiling was crushing his skull. He would die unless he went back to the hospital room. He tried to send his friends thought messages to say he had not forgotten them. His mouth was squashed up against the wall. He could breathe no longer. He willed himself to go back to Dolf and there was an unearthly shriek again.

Sam was back in the bed and the sheets were tucked in tightly around him. He had returned to real life and real time, but he was trapped just the same. And his eyes were still locked on Dolf's eyes, which were bigger than ever now. Sam had to resist staring into them. They were sucking at his soul.

Already his feet and legs felt as if they had turned to stone. But not his hands, not yet. With his right hand Sam could feel something – Dean's pistol – and he knew it was his only hope. He immediately formulated a plan. He would pretend to be dead, and then, when Dolf was least expecting it, he would fire the elixir in the pistol straight into his eyes. He made himself stop struggling and went limp.

An eternity passed. Slowly, carefully, so gradually Dolf would not notice, Sam reached for the water pistol, which was in his pyjama pocket. He found he was able to pull it up gradually inside the bedclothes. Focusing on what he was doing seemed to lessen the hold Dolf's eyes had over him. Then Sam gave a little sigh, pretending it was his last breath – ever. He hoped Dolf would think that he was no more.

Just as Sam wanted, Dolf came over to investigate. He was checking to see what had happened. Sam knew not to shut his eyes. He had seen films where people had died and their eyes stared open. So Sam put on a glazed look. And just as Dolf bent over him, he whipped out the water pistol and got Dolf right in the eye.

There was a bellow of rage so loud that Sam was sure the hospital staff would come running. Dolf's eyes glowed red. His shape began to change. Sam watched him, horrified. Dolf shook as if he was in unspeakable agony and there, in his place, stood a red-eyed wolf, baying at the moon. The wolf howled with sadness, and the howl diminished as the wolf's body became scaly. Now Dolf was a crocodile and his mouth was fixed in a slavering grin. He approached Sam's bed. He opened his jaw, and Sam thought, I must burn him up or he'll get me, and so he visualised blue flames enveloping the creature. The flames appeared in reality and licked at the crocodile's scales. There was a fizz and sizzle. The crocodile vanished. Now there was just a rat scurrying across the floor. As it reached the wall it became a fly and landed a metre above him, buzzing loudly.

At that moment Nurse Sebastian came in with a fly swatter and there was a juicy splat. All that was left of Dolf was a grisly smear on the wall.

'Dear, oh dear,' said Nurse Sebastian. 'We can't have flying insects in hospitals, Sam. They spread infection.'

'Nurse Sebastian!' came a shout from down the corridor. 'We need you in Room 5.'

Before Sam could speak to her, she had vanished.

Sam could hardly believe what had

happened. Dolf had not destroyed him, but he had destroyed Dolf. He was gone, all gone. Except for a nasty smear on the wall and his blue-tinted glasses, which were still on Sam's bedside table.

Curious, Sam picked up the glasses. Looking at them closely, he was surprised how thick the lenses were. They seemed to go on and on, like dark blue tunnels. There seemed to be light around the edges, like there is when you close your eyes very tightly. Sam stared at the blue so long he thought it was breaking up into a spectrum of colour. He was sorely tempted to put the glasses on. Would it be safe to do so? Would it bring Dolf back? Impossible. Sam had seen Dolf destroyed with his own eyes. So, very carefully, he hooked the frame over his ears and settled the glasses on the bridge of his nose. Sam blinked a few times. And stared into never-ending darkness.

As his eyes adjusted to the darkness, shapes swam into view. His body began to tingle and he felt as if he was rushing through space. He knew without a shred of doubt that he was back in Dolf's Dream Kingdom. At least, he was pretty certain it was Dolf's Dream Kingdom, because there were Hannah and Amy and Dean, still strapped to their chairs above the tank of snakes. Sam was filled with terror again. He took off the glasses so he could get a better view. To his surprise, Scipio, Piers and Gerontius seemed to be gone.

'Sam,' Hannah called out, her voice shaking. 'They're going to tip us into the snake pit.'

Ah, thought Sam, I must really be here, because Hannah can see me.

Sam advanced towards the tank. The sides were toughened Perspex and, sure enough, inside was a mass of green and gold snakes with forked red tongues. Sam looked again. The forked red tongues were made of felt. The snakes were not snakes at all, but doorstops.

'These aren't snakes,' he told his friends.

'But we saw them,' Amy said. 'Those three demons brought us in here and showed us. They were writhing and hissing and spitting at us. We were tied to the chairs and we were going to be eaten alive.'

'And then they all roared, the three ghosts,' Dean said. 'And each one turned into a snake, and then they got smaller and smaller. And then you came.'

Already Sam was untying his friends, and as he did so he explained about Dolf and the elixir. Hannah became very excited.

'You've done it, Sam! You've broken his power. I bet exactly at the moment he changed, Scipio and Piers and Gerontius did too. Because he was controlling them, you see. Dolf's gone from his own Dream Kingdom. So now we have to get to the Similator and squirt the rest of the elixir on it. And we'll have done it. Come on, come on. You're so clumsy, Sam. Here, let me!'

Hannah began to untie her own straps. Sam put Dolf's glasses in his pocket with the pistol.

Dean led them, running, into the central part of Dolf's Dream Kingdom. The shadow people were still there, all still walking, sitting, breathing in unison. The fact that Dolf and his cronies had been destroyed did not seem to affect them. They were still trapped in their shadow world, in an endless cycle of repetition and sameness. They had to be liberated, otherwise, Sam knew, he and his friends would have done only half a job. He prayed the Similator would be the key.

'The problem is,' said Hannah, 'that we don't know what we're looking for. What *is* the Similator? Have you ever seen it, Sam?'

'No,' Sam replied. 'I've seen the word on Dolf's computer, but that's all.'

'I guess it's some kind of machine,' Amy said. 'It's probably in a room by itself. And it has a ray-gun attachment or something.'

'Or it might be a sort of capsule and you have to stand in it,' said Hannah.

'No,' said Sam. 'If Dolf used it to change all the shadow people, he couldn't overpower them one at a time, which he'd have to do if he needed to put them in a capsule.'

The children were stuck. Sam hated the feeling. It reminded him of school, when you had an impossible maths problem, and the more you thought about it, the more impossible it seemed. But at least in school you could put up your hand and the teacher would come over. This time, they were on their own.

'How much elixir do you have left?' Hannah asked Sam.

'I don't know,' he said. 'Shall I have a look?'

Sam took the pistol out of his pocket. It didn't feel the same as it had when he'd aimed it at Dolf. Then it was heavy and metallic, like a real gun. Now it was plastic again. There were Dean's tooth marks on it. Sam experienced a dreadful sinking feeling.

'There's none left,' he said.

'You mean you used it all on Dolf?' Hannah said, worried.

'I didn't think I did, but . . . The inside of my pocket's all wet and sticky,' Sam continued.

'Maybe the elixir trickled out in your pocket,' Amy said slowly.

The children were all thinking the same – that if Amy was right, they could not destroy the Similator. They had no idea what the consequences of that would be.

'My pocket's all soaked,' Sam said miserably. 'The stuff's all over Dolf's glasses.'

He brought them out of his pocket. They glistened with the sticky remnants of what was the elixir. And all around them the trapped shadow people continued their interminable, regulated actions. Sam felt such a fool. He thought he had been so brave and clever, destroying Dolf, but stupidly he hadn't looked after the pistol properly and now the shadow people would be lost for ever. Not only that, but the real world would remain grey and lifeless.

'Never mind,' said Dean. 'Can I have a go with Dolf's glasses?'

Sam handed them to him despairingly and Dean put them on.

'Wheeeeeeeeeeeeeeeeee!!' Dean exclaimed.

The children ignored him. As usual, Dean was just being silly when there was a real problem that needed solving. Sam thought hard, his eyes on the ground. Maybe if they found the Similator and he put his damp pocket to it? Or ought they to go to Dolf's computer and try to break into the program he had seen?

He lifted his eyes to an astonishing sight. Several of the shadow people were no longer shadow people. They were not clad in drab overalls but dressed in normal, colourful clothes – red sweaters, patterned dresses. The women had coloured hair, some of them were grinning, some looked confused. But the most important thing was that they were all acting differently from each other.

'What's happening?' he shouted.

More and more people began to change. Then the transformations stopped. Dean took off the glasses. He handed them back to Sam.

'These are wizard, these specs. When you put them on, everyone turns kind of multi-coloured. It's like those 3D specs at the cinema. You know, when—'

Sam grabbed them from him and put them on. As he turned his head and looked at more and more shadow people, they changed in front of his eyes. One became a ballerina complete with tutu. Another was a Masai warrior.

'The glasses!' Sam shouted, frantic with joy.

'The *glasses* are the Similator! And they're full of elixir!'

He swivelled round and round and round. Everyone that he looked at changed. And they stayed changed, as Dean, Hannah and Amy could see them too. Inuits in sealskins, little old ladies in blue berets, ranch hands in battered denims, beautiful women in silk saris – all appeared before their eyes. And there was Rahila the acupuncturist in her orange silk scarf, and Mr Pearson, the Head, dressed for some reason as Father Christmas.

There was a babble of happy, excited voices talking in many different languages. There was music and a delicious aroma of different kinds of food, Sam thought. The hall was filled with sound. People were hugging and jumping, and he saw a traffic warden, a deep-sea diver and a very large opera singer giving a hippie the bumps.

'I've got it!' Hannah said. 'Whenever Dolf looked at someone, they became the same as everyone else, the same as his vision of them. But it didn't work on you, Sam, because of your Outsight. It didn't work on us either. Now we've reversed the glasses, we can use them in the other way – we can make people be themselves. Oh, this is so exciting. Yesssss!' Hannah shouted, sounding, for a moment, like Dean.

'Can I still be the MosquitoMan?' asked Dean.

Sam stared at him with the glasses on and for all of five minutes Dean was a tiny insect, buzzing around the girls' heads until they screamed for him to stop.

Sam suddenly had a thought. 'Sigmund! He might still be a prisoner. We must find him.'

As he thought it, he saw a door in front of them that seemed to glow as if it wanted to help them. The children shot through it, with Sam still wearing the glasses.

There was Sigmund's cell, but Sigmund was

no longer captive. Instead he was being hugged and his hand was being shaken by a number of men and women – seven, to be precise. They filled the cell with light and a rich, warming fragrance. Sam knew they were the other Dream Guardians. The sight of them filled his heart with joy.

'Well done, Sam, Hannah, Amy and Dean,' Sigmund said, smiling.

Nurse Sebastian was among them, this time clad in a golden robe that swept the ground.

'These are the children who put an end to Dolf, Scipio, Gerontius and Piers,' she said.

Sam could hear Carl's voice now. 'Yes. Four have gone and four have joined us.'

There was a muttering from the Dream Guardians, but Sigmund put a stop to it.

'There is yet more to do. I promise, we will meet again. But for now, go and conclude your work.'

'What does he mean?' Sam asked his friends.

'I know,' said Amy. 'Let's take the De-Similator to our Dream Kingdoms. Maybe it will change them back.'

'All together,' said Sam, shouting to be heard above the noise and laughter.

He wished to be back in his forest, wished as strongly as he had ever wished for anything. And there he was – there they were – and his forest was still bleak, cold and uninviting. But as he looked around with the spectacles on, it was like someone was there with a paint-brush, restoring the green and gold and woody browns. He saw what looked like dead greenbirds on the ground. As he stared at them through his glasses, with a flutter of wings they straightened themselves and began chirruping madly, their beaks clacking. Sam slowly turned in a circle. Everything that he looked at came back to life. He was filled with a happiness that threatened to make his heart burst. There was the Shooting Stone, the target brighter than ever. And a golden arrow had scored a bull's-eye. The multicoloured leaves chimed and rustled in the cool, balmy breeze. Over in the distance his river ran clear. All was well.

'Amy,' he said, offering her the glasses, 'it's your turn.'

Off they flew to Amy's Dream Kingdom. She circled above it, and Sam saw it regain its richness. He savoured the aroma of sweet and sour sauce. The ladies working on the sweet and sour conveyor belt saw the children above them, raised their heads and smiled. A dolphin somersaulted out of the water and placed a garland of seaweed around Amy's neck. Sam, Hannah and Dean cheered.

Then they sped off to Dean's kingdom and the glasses were handed to Dean. Each of his rides swung into action. And there, in the middle, was a new addition – a restaurant called the Oasis. There was a baboon selling hamburgers in coloured buns.

Dean gave the glasses to Hannah. She hesitated.

'My kingdom is different from yours. I don't want to go there. I don't see how the De-Similator can make it any better. It's only ever been nightmares.'

'Shall we try anyway?' Sam said. He didn't want her to feel left out.

'If you all come,' she said.

They held hands and were immediately back in Hannah's city. Black skyscrapers reached into the stormy, disturbed sky. Hannah put on the glasses and all the children turned in the direction she was looking. She peered into the lobby of the office block where they had taken the lift. It hadn't changed. They all walked with Hannah to the lift. It arrived empty, just as it had in their previous nightmare. Fighting their nerves, the children entered the lift. Sam saw their reflection in the mirror. He looked a little pale. Dean and Amy were the same. But then he noticed Hannah seemed different. Older and kind of better-looking. Sam didn't realise she could be like that. It made him feel funny.

The lift stopped, but when they got out it was to step into a luxurious hallway. A butler arrived with a silver tray on which were fruit cocktails. Smiling, he offered one to Hannah. All four children were ushered into a large penthouse apartment with breathtaking views. It was Hannah's apartment. They walked over to the window and saw a panorama of the city with a thousand golden lights twinkling, and neon lights, and car lights – a whole city, a whole world, alive and full of different people having different and exciting lives.

'I love it here,' Hannah said.

Sam saw that her face was alight with hope.

'It makes you feel,' she said, 'as if you could do anything. As if I could do anything. And there's no need to be afraid. Just lots of things to be found out and people to be discovered and . . . It makes me feel as if I want to grow up.'

'We've all started to grow up, I think,' Sam said. 'After what we've been through, we're not going to be the same again, are we?'

Amy agreed. But Dean had already jumped onto the creamy white sofa and had reached for the TV remote.

'You can invite me back here any time, Hannah,' he said. 'You've got hundreds and hundreds of channels!'

The children laughed, the tension broken.

'I think I might join you,' Hannah said to him. 'But first, Sam, take these.'

Carefully she handed the glasses back to him. They were precious now.

'Keep them safe,' she said.

'I certainly will,' Sam replied.

*

The next thing Sam knew, someone was telling him to wake up.

'Sam!' said the voice. 'Wake up! You've missed breakfast.'

It was his mother. Sitting by his hospital bed, she was dressed in her purple nightdress and pink dressing gown with the orchids on it.

'They let me spend the night here. I've been in the next room. They said you needed to sleep and I didn't want to wake you. Oh, Sam. I'm so glad you're OK!'

She bent over and kissed him, even though she knew he didn't really like being kissed all that much.

'I had such a strange dream last night,' she said. 'Really odd. I suppose it was because I was worried about you. There was a hippo playing a trombone and a wedding reception in a hot-air balloon. But I understand that bit. The wedding, I mean. You see, it's off. And I was going to let him know I'd come to my senses – and then I discovered he'd left without telling me! I must be crazy, Sam. I don't know what I could have seen in him. I really need to get a grip on myself.' She smiled. 'And here I am, rabbiting on about me and here you are with your concussion. Why don't we have a holiday when you're better? How about the seaside? With your friends, maybe? And I was looking at myself in the mirror before and I thought, Sam, I could do with an entirely new hairstyle – or maybe hair extensions. What do you . . . Oh, I'm so *glad* you're better!'

And she kissed him once again and, secretly, Sam didn't mind one bit.

The sky was bright blue outside his window. Nurse Sebastian came into his room with a tray with breakfast on it.

'I saved this for you,' she said. 'No eggs, I'm afraid.' She winked at him. 'But there's toast and lots of raspberry jam.'

'Now you must eat it all up,' his mother said. 'You'll need to get your strength back. And, nurse, I don't suppose I could make myself something to drink? I have my own camomile and kiwi fruit teabag with me.'

Nurse Sebastian said she'd see what she could do.

Sam's mother carried on beaming at him as he picked up a slice of toast. Suddenly he realised he was very, very hungry.

'I've decided,' she said, 'no more lodgers for us. Never, ever again. I'll find other ways of getting some extra income, don't you worry. I'm just so glad you're all right, Sam. You could have been – oh, I can't bear to think about it! What are these?' she asked suddenly, picking up Dolf's glasses. 'Haven't I—'

Sam reached out and grabbed them. 'A present from Hannah,' he improvised quickly. 'For an experiment. Science. I have to keep them safe.'

He put them in his washbag, and luckily the mention of Hannah sparked off a new train of thought for his mother.

'Hannah and your friends have been marvellous, Sam. They've been dying to visit you and would have stayed the night with me, but we sent them home. They've had to go to school today, but I promised them they could come round as soon as they let you out of hospital. Which Nurse Sebastian said could even be this afternoon, once the doctor has seen you. But I'll need to go and do some jobs first. There are some things I have to do. You'll be fine here. Shall I ask the nurse for some more toast, Sam?'

Sam, his mouth full, nodded vigorously

As soon as Sam stepped into his house, he knew it felt different. It was lighter and brighter, as if a burden had been lifted. Or maybe that was his imagination. What was certainly true was that his mother had been spring-cleaning.

'I've given the place a thorough clean,' she told him grimly. 'It needed it.'

And just then Sam thought he heard a familiar sound – a loud, insistent miaowing.

'Phoebe!' his mother exclaimed. 'She's come back!'

She ran to the kitchen and opened the back door. A rather thin, dirty-looking black and white cat shot in, and didn't stop her frantic miaowing until Sam's mum had put down a plate of food.

'I *wonder* where's she's been!' Sam's mum exclaimed. 'I bet she was trapped somewhere, or maybe she jumped into a lorry and had to find her way back. Who would have believed it? What an adventure!'

Sam bent down and stroked Phoebe's head. Then, leaving his mother pouring milk into a saucer, he went upstairs to his bedroom. As he reached the landing he noticed the door to what had been Dolf's room was standing open. Still a little scared, he made himself walk towards it. He looked in.

His mother had been very, very busy. All trace of the lodger had gone. Even the bed had been dismantled. Instead she had bought some beanbags, a little coffee table and a brightly coloured rug. On an old sideboard was a TV and a large picture of Grandma. In another corner was a huge plant. Sam's mother ran upstairs.

'Do you like it?' she asked, knowing that Sam would. 'I thought you could use it as a den. I think I'll get you a desk too. You could have friends to stay. Or maybe I could use it to practise my reflexology. What do you think?'

Sam just said, 'It looks . . . *so* much better.'

*

Later that night, as Sam's mum had promised, Hannah, Amy and Dean came round. Amy was clutching a brown paper bag from which a very inviting aroma was escaping.

'Sweet and sour chicken for all of us!' she announced. 'It's a present from my parents, Sam, to say sorry that you were knocked down and ended up in hospital. There's plenty for all of us.'

Sam's mum got some plates and soon they were eating away. Even Sam's mum helped herself to a little chicken, but then said she thought the children might like to be alone together.

'If it was the weekend,' she said, 'I'd let you stay over, but there's school tomorrow.' She vanished into the kitchen.

'This is delicious,' Dean said, shoving a whole fried chicken ball in his mouth, so that he looked like a hamster with one cheek puffed out.

'And guess what?' Amy said. 'My parents have put back all the old dishes and added some more. We have a bigger menu than any other takeaway in the area.'

'Yes,' said Hannah. 'Everything's gone back

to normal and is better than ever. I know I'm contradicting myself, but it's true. Katie and Lauren and Emma and Claire! Listen to this! They've had a big row and fallen out. They all came to school this morning wearing different clothes. Lauren asked if she could go around with me!'

'Did you say yes?' asked Sam. He was worried. After all they'd gone through, he didn't want to lose Hannah.

'Don't be silly,' Hannah said. 'I belong here. And I've brought you your school books, Sam, so you can catch up on the work you've missed.'

'Thanks, Hannah,' Sam said, with all the sarcasm he could muster.

'I can't wait for you to get better,' she said, smiling. 'The world feels so good now.'

'I *am* better,' Sam said. 'The doctor at the hospital said I escaped very lightly. But he did say I could have the rest of the week off school – which can't be bad!'

'But school is nice now,' Amy said. 'Mr Pearson said there's going to be a drama festival and Year 7 can do a pantomime and there's going to be auditions. I've put my name down. Mr Pearson has promised me a part. He stopped me in the corridor and we talked about it.'

Sam glanced at Hannah and smiled. What she had said was true. Things weren't just back to normal, but better. It made him think that all the terrifying adventures they had shared were probably for the good, in some mysterious way. But his head hurt when he tried to puzzle out what it all meant. He was glad when Dean interrupted his thoughts.

'I've got you a video of *Batman*,' said Dean. 'Because – look – if we're gonna be superheroes, we'd better start learning.'

'That's the bit that puzzles me,' Sam replied. 'Are we going to be Dream Guardians now, or use our Outsight again? Or has our adventure finished? Dolf is no more, so all the danger is over.'

'I don't know about you, Sam,' Hannah said, 'but I'd like a bit of a rest. I'm glad Dolf has gone. But in the future, if ever we could help . . .'

'Yeah!' shouted Dean. 'Sam and Hannah and Amy and MosquitoMan to the rescue! Bzzzzzzzzzzzzzzz!'

'Who knows?' said Amy.

Hannah smiled, speared a piece of chicken with her plastic fork, dipped it in the sauce and popped it in Sam's mouth. As Sam chewed, he thought he didn't mind what the future would bring, or how it might change him. He'd be OK because he had the best friends in all the world.

Do you remember what you dream?
Some people believe your dreams
can predict the future.

Believe it or not, if you dream of . . .

An aeroplane – you are about to hear news from a person or place far away.

An alarm – there's an exciting time ahead of you.

Aliens – big changes are on the way.

Angels – you will enjoy success, happiness and good friendships.

Balloons – you might have some small disappointments.

Bees – bees buzzing means good news, stinging bees mean good fortune.

Birds – singing, flying or brightly-coloured birds are all good omens in dreams.

Bubbles – certain worries are about to disappear. If you are making the bubbles, be careful about spending too much money.

A burglar – you are likely to come into some money.

A car accident – you are likely to recover something you've lost.

A camera – beware of false friends.

A ruined castle – you need to watch your temper.

A cat – if you chased the cat away, expect a stroke of good luck.

Cheese – you'll have good luck.

Chewing gum – this means you shouldn't tell all your secrets to a new friend.

Chocolate – you will enjoy a good health.

Christmas – to dream about Christmas out of season means happy family times ahead.

Climbing – look forward to success or prosperity.

Dogs – they symbolise friends and are a good omen, unless they are biting or attacking you!

Elephants – a great sign of good luck in dreams.

An explosion – this signifies a big improvement in your life.

Falling – you feel your life might be out of control. Get organised.

A fight – a change lies ahead for you.

Fire – putting out a fire suggests you will overcome obstacles in your life.

Flowers – fresh or bright flowers are a sign of happiness in your life.

Football – playing football in your dream suggests you may come into some money.

Ghosts – relax! Seeing a ghost in your dream is a sign of good luck, unless the ghost scares you, in which case it means you should resist pressure to do something you're not happy with.

Holes – digging a hole means a trip is on the horizon, falling into one means you should watch out for nasty friends.

Icebergs – a dream about an iceberg means an obstacle ahead.

Kidnap – if you dream about being kidnapped, you may be embarrased about your group of friends. Try making some new ones!

A ladder – climbing a ladder signifies a great achievement. If you fell off it, though, you may be trying too hard at something.

Magic – dreaming about magic signifies unexpected changes in your life.

The ocean – an ocean journey means an escape from an irritating problem. A calm sea is a good sign, a choppy one a sign of mixed fortune.

An operation – you will go through important life-changes.

Pirates – this is an indication that you are looking for adventure.

The police – dreaming about the police signifies security and safety in you life.

A postman – there's news on the way.

Roses – picking roses is a sign of joy to come, giving them means you are well-loved, receiving them means you will be popular.

Spiders – are a sign of good luck. To kill one in your dream is good news, to watch one spinning a web means you will be rich!

Strangers – you will soon be reunited with good friends.

Television – if you dreamt about last night's TV programmes, it means you're watching too much telly! Try reading a book instead.

Thunder – is a sign that your problems will soon be solved.

Treasure – digging for treasure is a sign of good health, finding it a sign of good fortune.

Warts – warts on your hands in a dream is a sign of money to come – the more warts, the more money!

A witch – a witch in your dream means fun social times ahead.

A zoo – new places and new faces are ahead of you.